KINGFISHER • *TREASURIES*

Ideal for reading aloud with younger children, or for more experienced readers to enjoy independently, Kingfisher *Treasuries* offer the very best writing for children. Carefully chosen by expert compilers, the selection in each book is varied and wide-ranging. There are modern stories, traditional folk tales and fables, stories from a variety of cultures around the world, as well as work from exciting contemporary authors.

Popular with both children and their parents, the books in the *Treasury* series provide a useful introduction to new authors and encourage children to take pleasure in reading.

KINGFISHER
Larousse Kingfisher Chambers Inc.
95 Madison Avenue
New York, New York 10016

First edition 1996
2 4 6 8 10 9 7 5 3 1

LIBRARY OF CONGRESS CATALOGING-IN-PUBLICATION DATA
A treasury of ghost stories /
Kenneth Ireland [compiler] : Tony Morris [illustrator].
p. cm.
Summary: A collection of scary and humorous ghost stories, both traditional and contemporary, by such authors as Dick King-Smith, Margaret Mahy, Robert Swindells, and Catherine Storr.
1. Ghost stories. 2. Children's stories. [1. Ghosts—Fiction.
2. Short stories.] I. Ireland, Kenneth II. Morris, Tony, Ill.
PZ5.T7526 1996 [Fic]—dc20 96–1907 CIP AC

ISBN 0–7534–5027–5

Printed in Great Britain

Acknowledgments

The publisher would like to thank the copyright holders for permission to reproduce the following copyright material:

Joan Aiken: A.M. Heath & Co. Ltd. for "Beezlebub's Baby" from *A Foot in the Grave* by Joan Aiken, Jonathan Cape Ltd. 1989. Copyright © Joan Aiken Enterprises Ltd 1989. **Barbee Oliver Carleton**: Highlights for Children, Inc. Columbus, Ohio for "Gabriel" by Barbee Oliver Carleton. Copyright © Highlights for Children, Inc. **Kevin Crossley-Holland**: Scholastic Children's Books for "The Dauntless Girl" from *The Dead Moon* by Kevin Crossley-Holland, André Deutsch 1982. Copyright © Kevin Crossley-Holland 1982. **Cynthia C. DeFelice**: "The Dancing Skeleton" adapted by Cynthia C. DeFelice from "David Aaron II" by John Bennett copyright © John Bennett 1946, renewed 1974, published with the permission of Russell and Volkening. **Grace Hallworth**: Reed Consumer Books Ltd. for "The Headless Rider" from *Mouth Open, Story Jump Out* by Grace Hallworth, Methuen Children's Books 1984. Copyright © Grace Hallworth 1984. **Kenneth Ireland**: The author for "The Shortest Ghost Story Ever Told," "The Second Shortest Ghost Story Ever Told," and "Tommy and the Ghost." Copyright © Kenneth Ireland 1996. **Dick King-Smith**: A.P. Watt Ltd. for "The Ghost at Codlin Castle" from *The Ghost at Codlin Castle and Other Stories* by Dick King-Smith, Viking 1992. Copyright © Fox Busters Ltd. 1992. **Margaret Mahy**: J.M. Dent for "Looking for a Ghost" from *The Third Margaret Mahy Story Book* by Margaret Mahy, J.M. Dent 1975. Copyright © Margaret Mahy 1975. **Ruth Manning-Sanders**: David Higham Associates Ltd. for "Hans and his Master" from *A Book of Ghosts and Goblins* by Ruth Manning-Sanders, Methuen Children's Books 1968. Copyright © Ruth Manning-Sanders 1968. **Susan Price**: A.M. Heath & Co. Ltd. for "The Errand" from *Ghosts at Large* by Susan Price, Faber & Faber 1984. Copyright © Susan Price 1984. **Robert D. San Souci**: Doubleday, a division of Bantam Doubleday Dell Publishing Group Inc. for "The Ghost of Misery Hill" from *Short and Shivery: Thirty Chilling Tales* by Robert D. San Souci. Copyright © Robert D. San Souci 1987. **Dinah Starkey**: Reed Consumer Books Ltd. for "The Laying of the Pakenham Ghost" from *Ghosts and Bogles* by Dinah Starkey, William Heinemann Ltd. Copyright © Dinah Starkey 1978. **Catherine Storr**: Lutterworth Press for "Bill's Ghost" by Catherine Storr from *Ghosts and Shadows*, edited by Dorothy Edwards, Lutterworth Press 1980. Copyright © Catherine Storr 1980. **Robert Swindells**: Jennifer Luithlen Agency for "Night School" by Robert Swindells. Copyright © Robert Swindells 1984, 1995.

Every effort has been made to obtain permission to reproduce copyright material but there may be cases where we have been unable to trace a copyright holder. The publisher will be happy to correct any omissions in future printings.

A • TREASURY • OF GHOST STORIES

CHOSEN BY
Kenneth Ireland

ILLUSTRATED BY
Tony Morris

Kingfisher
NEW YORK

CONTENTS

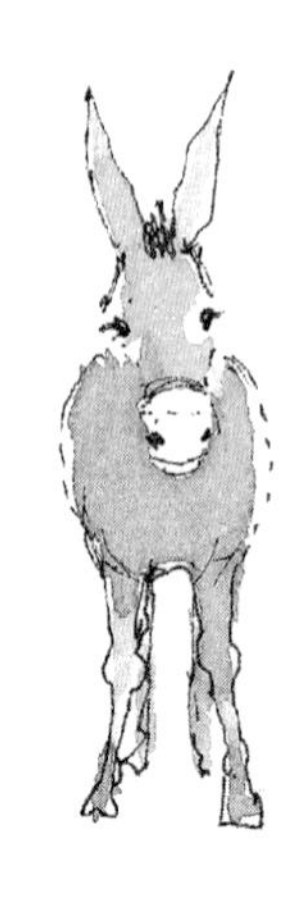

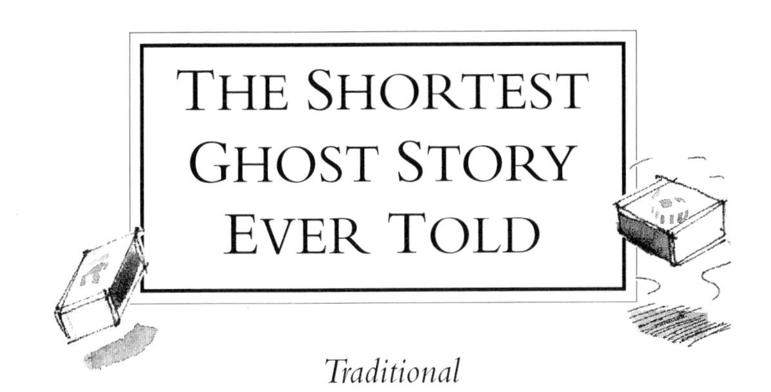

The Shortest Ghost Story Ever Told

Traditional

He woke up frightened, and reached for the matches, and the matches were put into his hand.

THE GHOST AT CODLIN CASTLE

Dick King-Smith

"Gran," said Peter as his grandmother was tucking him up in bed, "d'you believe in ghosts?"

"Oh yes," said his grandmother.

"So d'you know a good ghost story to tell me?"

"Now?"

"Yes."

"All right."

Like a great many ghosts (said Gran), Sir Anthony Appleby was wary of people. It wasn't that they could do him any harm. That had been done ages ago. It was the fuss they made when they came upon him, in the winding corridors and steep stone stairways of Codlin Castle.

Some screamed and ran, some stood rooted to the spot, trembling and ashen-faced, some fainted.

But no one ever said a kind word to him. In fact, no one had spoken a word of any kind to him since his death in 1588. In time past, things had not been so bad, for then the only inhabitants of Codlin Castle had been the Appleby family and their servants; all were quite used to the ghost of Sir Anthony, and though they may not have spoken to him, at least they were no trouble to him.

Nowadays things were different, for the Appleby fortunes had dwindled over the centuries, until finally one of Sir Anthony's descendants had been forced to sell the family seat.

Now it was known as the Codlin Castle Hotel, where well-to-do folk came to stay, to sleep in canopied four-posters and to eat rich meals in the medieval Banqueting Hall. Sir Anthony kept bumping into them in the corridors and stairways, and all of them, it seemed, were frightened of ghosts.

"A fellow can't get any peace these days," said Sir Anthony grumpily (like all ghosts, he talked to himself a great deal). "One look at me and they lose their heads," and then he allowed himself a smile, for though dressed in the costume of his age —doublet and hose, flowing cloak, high ruffed collar, sword by his side—he was, as always, carrying his head underneath one arm.

For three hundred and forty-two years he had carried it thus, ever since that fateful day when, as one of her courtiers, he had accompanied Queen Elizabeth on a visit to her fleet at Tilbury.

On the dockside there was a large puddle, and the Queen stopped before it.

"Your cloak, Sir Anthony," she said.

Sir Anthony hesitated.

"Majesty?" he said.

"I may have the heart and stomach of a king," said Queen Elizabeth, "but I have the feet of a weak and feeble woman and I don't want to get them wet. Cast your cloak upon yonder puddle."

"But Your Majesty," said Sir Anthony Appleby, "it is a brand-new cloak and it will get all muddy," at which the Queen ordered that he be taken straight away to the Tower of London and there beheaded, while Sir Walter Raleigh hastily threw down his own cloak.

The years and indeed the centuries slipped by. One sultry summer's night in 1930, the stable clock was striking twelve as the ghost made his way along a stone-flagged passageway in the West Wing, his head tucked underneath his left arm. This was how he usually carried it, to leave his sword-arm free, though sometimes he changed sides, for the head was quite heavy. Once, a couple of hundred years ago, he had tried balancing it on top of his neck, just for fun, but this had not been a success. A serving-wench had come upon him suddenly in the castle kitchens, making him jump so that the

head fell off and rolled along the floor, at which the wretched girl, a newcomer, had died of fright.

Remembering this incident as the twelfth stroke sounded, Sir Anthony stopped opposite a tall cheval glass standing in the passage, and taking up his head with both hands, set it carefully above the great ruffed collar.

"A fine figure of a man," he remarked to his reflection, "though I say it myself," and, pressing his palms against his ears to keep the head steady, he turned this way and that, the better to admire himself. He could not therefore hear the approach of soft footsteps, but suddenly saw, beside his own reflection, that of a small girl in pink pajamas.

"Hello," she said. "Who are you?"

So startled was Sir Anthony that he almost dropped his head.

"My . . . my name is . . . is Sir Anthony Appleby," he stammered, turning to face the child. "And who, pray, are you, young miss?"

"I'm Biffy," said the small girl. "It's short for Elizabeth."

That name again, thought Sir Anthony, but at least someone's spoken to me at last.

"Why aren't you in bed?" he said.

"Too hot," said Biffy. "I couldn't sleep. Why aren't you?"

"Oh, I never sleep," said Sir Anthony. "I'm a ghost, you see."

"What fun," said Biffy. "How long have you been dead?"

"Three hundred and forty-two years."

"Oh. So that's why you're wearing those funny clothes."

"Yes."

"Why have you got your hands pressed to your ears? Have you the earache?"

"No, no," said Sir Anthony. "Ghosts can't feel pain. It's about the only advantage of being one."

"Then why are you holding your head?" said Biffy.

Oh dear, thought the ghost. If I take off my head, the child will scream or faint or even die of fright. And I do so want her to say a kind word to me. One kind word and I'm sure I could rest in peace at long last, instead of having to trudge around these winding corridors and steep stone stairways for the rest of my death.

"Look," he said. "If I tell you a secret, will you promise faithfully not to scream or faint or die of fright?"

"I promise."

"Well, you see, when I died, it was in a rather unusual way. I mean, it was common enough then, but they don't do it nowadays."

"What did they do to you?"

"They executed me. They cut off my head. That's why I'm holding it like this now. I'm just balancing it, you see. It's not attached."

"What fun," said Biffy. "Take it off."

The ghost's face wore a very worried expression.

"You promised not to scream or faint or die of fright, remember?" he said.

"Yes," said Biffy. "Don't worry."

So Sir Anthony Appleby removed his head, holding it carefully by its long hair, and tucked it under his arm.

The small girl in the pink pajamas clapped her hands in delight.

"That's wonderful!" she said, and at these words a broad grin of pleasure spread over the bearded features.

"Oh, Sir Anthony Appleby," said Biffy. "You really are the nicest ghost in the whole wide world!" and because she was just the right height, she gave him a kiss on the top of his head.

Immediately the ghost of Codlin Castle vanished.

Biffy looked all around, but there was no sign of him.

She looked in the cheval glass, but saw only her

own reflection, standing there in her pink pajamas.

So she went back to bed.

"Is that the end of the story?" said Peter.

"Yes, I suppose it is," said his grandmother. "Except that from then onward, nobody at the Codlin Castle Hotel ever saw the ghost of Sir Anthony Appleby again."

"Because he was at peace at last, you mean?"

"Yes."

"Because the girl said a kind word to him?"

"Yes."

"Gran," said Peter. "Your name's Elizabeth, isn't it?"

"Yes. But when I was little, I was always called Biffy."

THE DANCING SKELETON

An African-American tale retold by
Cynthia C. DeFelice

Aaron Kelly was dead.

There wasn't anything anybody could do about it. And, to tell you the truth, nobody much cared. Aaron had been so downright mean and ornery in his life that folks were glad to see him go. Even his widow never shed a tear. She just bought a coffin, put Aaron in it, and buried him. Goodbye, Aaron Kelly, and good riddance!

But that very night, Aaron got up out of his grave, walked through the graveyard, and came home. His widow was sitting in the parlor, thinking how peaceful and quiet it was without Aaron around, when he walked right in the door.

"What's all this?" he shouted. "You're all dressed in black. You look like somebody died. Who's dead?"

The widow pointed a shaking finger at Aaron.

"You are!" she said.

"Oh, no, I ain't!" hollered Aaron. "I don't feel dead. I feel fine!"

"Well, you don't look fine," said the widow. "You look dead! Now you just get yourself back in that coffin where you belong."

"Oh, no," said Aaron. "I ain't goin' back to that coffin till I feel dead."

Just plain ornery, he was.

Well, since Aaron wouldn't go back to the grave, his widow couldn't collect the life insurance. Without that money, she couldn't pay for the coffin. If she didn't pay for the coffin, the undertaker might take it back. And if he did that, she'd *never* be rid of Aaron! Aaron didn't care. He just sat in his favorite rocking chair, rocking back and forth, back and forth, day after day, night after night. But after a while, Aaron began to dry up. Pretty soon he was nothing but a skeleton.

Every time he rocked, his old bones clicked and clacked. His widow did her best to ignore him, but it wasn't easy with all the racket he made.

Then one night, the best fiddler in town came to call on Aaron's widow. He'd heard Aaron was dead, and he thought he might marry the woman himself.

The fiddler and the widow sat down together, cozylike, on the bench . . . and ole Aaron sat right

across from them, just a-creakin' and a-crackin' and a-grinnin'. Fiddler said, "Woman, how long am I going to have to put up with that old bag o' bones sitting there? I can't court you proper with him staring at me like that!" Widow answered, "I know! But what can we do?"

The fiddler shrugged. The widow sighed. The clock ticked. And Aaron rocked. Finally, Aaron said, "Well, *this* ain't any fun at all. Fiddler, take out your fiddle. I feel like dancin'!"

So the fiddler took out his fiddle and began to play. My, my! He could make that fiddle sing!

Aaron Kelly heard that sweet music and he couldn't sit still. He stood up. Oooh, his dry bones felt stiff! He stretched himself. He shook himself. He cracked his knucklebones—aaah! And he began to dance.

With his toe bones a-tappin' and his feet bones a-flappin', round and round he danced like a fool! With his finger bones a-snappin' and his arm bones a-clappin', how that dead man did dance!

The music grew wilder, and so did Aaron until, suddenly, a bone broke loose from that dancing skeleton, flew through the air, and landed on the floor with a CLATTER!

"Oh, my!" cried the fiddler. "Look at that! He's dancing so hard, he's *falling apart!*"

"Well, then," said the widow, "*play faster!*"

The fiddler played faster.

Bones began flying every which way, and still that skeleton danced!

"*Play louder!*" cried the widow.

The fiddler hung on to that fiddle. He fiddled a tune that made the popcorn pop. He fiddled a tune that made the bedbugs hop. He fiddled a tune that made the rocks get up and dance! Crickety-crack, down and back!

Old Aaron went a-hoppin', his dry bones a-poppin'. Flippin' and floppin', they just kept droppin'!

Soon there was nothing left of Aaron but a pile

of bones lying still on the floor . . . all except for his old bald head bone, and *that* looked up at the fiddler, snapped its yellow teeth, and said,

"O O O O O W E E E ! AIN'T WE HAVING FUN!"

It was all too much for the fiddler. He dropped his fiddle, said, "Woman, I'm getting out of here!" and ran out the door. The widow gathered up Aaron's bones and carried them back to the graveyard. She put them in the coffin and mixed them all around in there, so Aaron could never put himself back together.

After that, Aaron Kelly stayed in his grave where he belonged.

But folks say that if you walk by the graveyard on a still summer night when the crickets are fiddling their tunes, you'll hear a faint clicking and clacking down under the ground.

And you'll know . . . it's Aaron's bones, still trying to dance.

And what about the fiddler and the widow?

Well, they never did get together again. Aaron Kelly had made DEAD SURE of that!

THE LAYING OF THE PAKENHAM GHOST

An English folktale retold by Dinah Starkey

It was in the days when Parson Andrews was a young curate that the Pakenham ghost began to walk. It was a very common or garden type of ghost—so ordinary, in fact, that nobody even knew who it was. But it haunted a farmhouse near Pakenham in Suffolk, and a great nuisance it made of itself.

It was a noisy ghost. It banged and thumped and slammed doors. The farmer and his wife would hear its hollow groans overhead, always when they were getting off to sleep. When it was feeling above itself it broke china, too. It bounced it off the dresser and smashed it on the floor.

The farmer's wife, who was a good-natured woman, had a kindness for the ghost.

"Poor thing," she said. "And wouldn't you feel sorry for yourself, flapping around in a sheet with

never a bite to keep out the cold?"

But the farmer, who was a harder case, said it had only got its just deserts. "Stands to reason," he said. "It must have done something wrong during its life to get itself ghosted."

The farmer's wife ruled in that household, however, and she decided to cure the ghost by kindness.

"Make it feel at home," she explained. "Then it won't need to go racketing around waking people up."

She took to laying a knife and fork for it at every meal and chatting to it about the weather. The rest of the household didn't fancy the idea at all. The plowboy said it gave him the willies not knowing whether anything was there or not, and the farmer reckoned his pudding never lay easy. But it did seem to do the trick. For a time it looked as if the ghost was settling down.

Then the effort got too much for it. After a month or two of best behavior it started getting up to its old tricks again. And this time the farmer put his foot down.

"I'm not having another broken night whatever you say, Mother. That ghost's got to go."

So he sent for the parson to get rid of it and the parson turned up carrying bell, book, and candle and bringing with him his curate, the young Mr. Andrews. He was as downy as a day-old chick, Mr. Andrews, and he'd never even seen a ghost, let alone laid one.

"Now then," said old Parson Clegg, "it's all very well reading the thing down but where are you going to put it after that?"

"Put it?" said the farmer blankly.

"Of course. I can shrink it down for you but that doesn't get rid of it altogether. We need a place for it—somewhere it can't get out of . . ." He paused and, seeing the farmer still looked uncertain, added, "The usual place is a bottle."

"Ah!" said the farmer, his face clearing. "Well, I should think I could . . ."

"Oh no you don't," his wife interrupted. "I'm not having that poor thing squashed up in any old bottle. No, if you've got to be rid of it—and I still think it's a pity—then it can go in the spare room wardrobe, which is nice and roomy."

"But I keep my Sunday best in there!" protested the farmer.

"For shame!" said his wife. "Grudging the poor creature a decent home. The cupboard it shall be."

With that settled, the laying began. They had a hard time with that ghost. It liked the farmhouse and having its own knife and fork and it didn't want to go. Parson Clegg read till his voice was hoarse and had the young curate spinning around like a teetotum, lighting candles and putting them out, ringing bells, and swinging dishes of sweet-smelling herbs. But the old parson had read down a lot of ghosts in his time and before the day was out

he'd got it shrunk to the size of a fieldmouse and laid it in the cupboard with the key on the outside. The farmer papered the door over so neatly you'd scarcely know it was there, and nothing was heard of the ghost for a long time.

Years went by and the house changed hands. A new couple took it over, who came from Norfolk. Nobody told them about the ghost because they were a nice young couple and nobody wanted to bother them. But one day as the wife—Alice Willcox, her name was—dusted out the bedroom, she happened to notice a bump in the wallpaper. It was where the key stuck out, in fact, but she didn't know that. She called one of the maids, who'd been there in the old farmer's time, and asked what it was.

"A cupboard, ma'am," said the maid unwillingly.

"Well I never!" said Alice. "Help me to pull off the wallpaper then."

"No!" said the maid. "I wouldn't do that!"

"Why ever not?" Alice was stripping off the paper as she spoke, and she'd found the lock.

"Don't! Leave it alone!"

But Alice had got the key free and she was turning it.

"There's a ghost, ma'am!"

"A ghost? What nonsen . . ."

But as she spoke she opened the door and with a whoosh and a blast of freezing air, the ghost got

out. A cloud of mist formed in the air, whirled and went streaking upstairs. There was a furious banging and a crash. It was back in business.

Down flew the plowman to the vicarage to root out the parson.

"Come quick!" he panted. "The ghost's got out and it's breaking up the house!"

Young curate Andrews, who was now Parson Andrews, and quite a few years older, sighed. He remembered that long hard day with the bell and the candles. But he got his things together and ran.

The ghost was bashing about in the attic, and the dairymaid was having hysterics. There wasn't a whole piece of china in the house.

"Put it back at once!" cried Alice Willcox. "It's gone mad!"

The ghost let out a howl like a banshee, and Parson Andrews gritted his teeth.

"Back in the cupboard?" he asked wearily.

"No," she said. "Not there. It'll only get out again. And I must say," she added, "it was a pretty silly place to put a ghost in the first place. Asking for trouble."

"I did hear tell," put in the maid, "of a ghost being locked up in a clock once. Now we've got that old grandfather clock down in the hall and it's never gone right since the old farmer knocked it over."

"The very thing," said Parson Andrews. "I'll put it in the pendulum."

"Yes," said Alice Willcox, "and before you know it, someone'll come along and open it up again. No. You take the pendulum and put it somewhere safe."

"Down the well," said Parson Andrews. "Now, may I begin?"

And so the ghost was laid. Parson Andrews wrestled with it all afternoon but, as night was falling, the ghost gave a final howl and squeezed into the pendulum slick as butter. And they took it and dropped it right to the bottom of the well and put the cover on the well and a stone on top of that.

"And if it gets out now," said Parson Andrews, "I'll eat my hat."

Time passed and Alice Willcox grew tired of farming, with the mud and the pigs and a ghost down the well. So she and her husband went back to Norfolk and they sold the farm to old Mr. Greenman, who'd had his eye on it for years. He knew all about the ghost, of course, but he rented it to a man called Bateson and he didn't let on.

Before Bateson had been in a month, he decided to drag the well. You'd be surprised at the things that were down there. Bateson found a rusty tea kettle, two buckets, half a dozen bed-springs and, last of all, a dull metal object that looked like a pendulum. And that pleased him very much because he'd noticed the clock in the hall didn't work and this had annoyed him. He took it back to the house, cleaned it up and hung it inside the clock again. Then he gave the screw a couple of turns and set it going.

There was a groan of rusty cogs creaking into action. The clock gave one slow, heavy tick and then, with a swoop and a cloud of smoke, the ghost was out of the clock and racing through the kitchen. There was a rattle and a violent cry and before Bateson knew what had hit him, the ghost was back.

He couldn't make head nor tail of it. Nobody told him the house was haunted. But he was no man's fool and he had the stable lad out and down to the vicarage before you could say Jack Robinson.

Old Parson Andrews was shaky now, and rather deaf, but he didn't need telling twice. Not where the ghost was concerned.

"This is too much!" he said. "Sheer carelessness! Am I to spend the rest of my days bundling that ghost back into captivity? And where am I to put it this time? In a cheese cloth, I suppose. Or perhaps your master would prefer the four-poster?"

"Dunno, sir," said the stable lad woodenly.

"Very well. But I warn you, boy, this is the last time!"

He hobbled down to the farm, clutching his bell, book, and candle. The ghost was racketing about in the kitchen and old Parson Andrews fairly let fly at it.

"Hold your peace, sir!" he stormed. "As if you haven't caused enough trouble already. And as for you, farmer," he turned on Bateson, "I must say you'd have done better to leave things alone. Still, it's no good crying over spilt milk. I can put it down the well again, but if I do, I want it sealed up properly. I really cannot go through this performance again."

"Oh, I'll seal it up, sir," said Bateson grimly. "I'll block the well with good solid stone, and that's a promise."

"Good!" said Parson Andrews and he rounded on the ghost. He hunted it through the house, trapped it in a corner, and then drove it backward, step by step, till it was hard up against the well. It didn't stand a chance. The parson was in such a fury he could have tackled the Wild Hunt single-handed. He got it into the well in ten minutes flat. There was a bad-tempered yelp and the ghost was gone.

"I leave it in your hands," he told Bateson. "But if you take my advice you'll use mortar, good and thick."

But in the end, Bateson did better. He filled in the well as he had promised and he built a summerhouse on top. It was a funny looking summerhouse because the walls were six foot thick and the door was triple bolted.

"But it'll stand till Judgment Day," he said. "And as for getting out, I'd just like to see the varmint try!"

And it never did. Not so far, anyway. But if you happen to be around Pakenham way and you come across a very solid looking summerhouse . . . watch your step.

NIGHT SCHOOL

Robert Swindells

Things had started to go missing from school recently, just little things like pencils and rulers, so far. They seemed to vanish overnight, which was odd, so when Lucy's mother found that Lucy had left her leotard at school that Friday, she wasn't very pleased.

"You must go straight back and fetch it," she said, even though it was nearly seven o'clock by then. "It's not far, so don't be long."

Lucy's friend Jen was with her, so they went together. By the time they reached the school gates the porch light was on, and light showed through one small window too, but most of the place was in darkness.

Jen nodded toward the lighted window. "That'll be Mrs. Berry, the caretaker, but the cleaners will have gone. Come on."

They hurried into school and were just about to cross the dark hall when Lucy seized Jen's sleeve and pointed.

"Look!"

On the far side of the hall a classroom door was opening and two shadowy figures appeared. They looked like children, except that their heads seemed too big and glowed faintly green. As the friends watched, the two figures went back into the classroom, closing the door behind them.

"They're just kids," Jen breathed.

"Are you sure?" whispered Lucy. "Those oversize heads, sort of glowing?"

"Sure," Jen replied. "They're not ghosts or monsters, if that's what you mean. They're people. *I'm* not scared of them—are you?"

"A bit," admitted Lucy. "But my leotard's in that room. Will you go first, Jen?"

Jen took a deep breath and strode across the hall with Lucy at her heels. She would fling open the door, and then they would see what they would see. After all, these creatures had no business here, creeping about in the dark. Whoever they were, they'd be as scared of Lucy and herself as the girls were of them—more scared, probably.

The door had a small glass panel, and through it the girls could see figures moving about in the gloom. Then they must have heard a noise, because all the figures froze. There was a clatter and scrape of chairs as Jen bravely flung back the door and switched on the lights.

They both blinked at the sudden brightness. But when they opened their eyes again—the figures had gone! Books, pencils, and sheets of paper lay on some of the tables, the chairs stood higgledy-piggledy and two had fallen over, but there was nobody there at all. At least Lucy's leotard was still there, folded up neatly on her table. She picked it up.

"But they were here!" Jen cried. "You saw them, didn't you?"

Lucy gulped and nodded. "Yes. There were at least six. They must have been ghosts, Jen—only ghosts could vanish like that."

Jen shook her head. "Ghosts don't read books or knock chairs over. They were real, like you and me, only . . . Can you hear something?" Lucy listened. Somewhere, water was running. "Somebody's in the washrooms. Come on!"

She switched off the lights again, then they tiptoed out of the classroom and toward the washrooms.

Lucy stopped. "It's coming from the boys' side," she whispered. "We can't go in there."

"Of course we can. You don't think there'll be boys there at this time of night, do you?"

They crept through the open doorway and peered around the corner. A shadowy form bent over the end washbasin, washing its hands. Close to where they stood a chair was against the wall. On the chair was a large, roundish object that glowed faintly green.

"Oh Jen—look," moaned Lucy. "It's taken its head off."

"No it hasn't. It's some sort of helmet. I bet they all wear them—that's what makes their heads look so big."

"So what should we do?"

"This." Before Lucy could protest, Jen had switched on the lights.

It was a boy. At least, it looked like a boy. He was dark-haired and slender, and about the same height as Lucy. His eyes were dark and his skin a yellowish brown. He wore black jeans and silver sneakers and a black, quilted jacket with the sleeves rolled up. As the washroom flooded with light he stared at the two girls, then past them to where the helmet rested on the chair.

"Who are you?" asked Jen.

"Kit." The boy's eyes were on the helmet.

"Where are you from?"

"Not where. When. Gimme headgear."

Jen shook her head. "Not till you tell us where you come from and what you're doing in our school."

"My school, too. Your school, 1995. My school, 2495. Five hundred years from now, yes?"

Jen's eyes narrowed. "Are you saying you're from the future?"

"Print that."

"Pardon?"

"Sorry. I mean yes, that's right."

"We don't believe you, do we Lucy?"

Lucy nodded rather nervously.

"I can't make you believe me. Okay if I dry?"

"Sure." Jen nodded toward the helmet. "You can have this in a minute."

He walked away from them and dried his hands under the hand-dryer.

When the dryer stopped and he tugged down his sleeves—"Where did the others go?" asked Lucy quietly.

"Back."

"Where? I mean, one second they were there, the next they'd vanished. How did they do that?"

"Escape key," said Kit. He pointed to the helmet. "In there."

"Oh. Is that why you didn't vanish too?"

"Print that. 'Headgear will be worn at all times.' A rule. I broke the rule. Nokay?"

"Nokay?"

"Nokay. That means stupid. Thick, yes?"

Both girls nodded, smiling.

"You," said Kit. "Why you here at night?"

"We came to collect my leotard," said Lucy. "Before it got moved, or disappeared," she added pointedly.

"Moved is not okay," said Kit, frowning. "Disappear is not okay. The rule says, 'Nothing to be taken away from its time or place.' But some kids break the rules. It's rom."

"What's rom?"

Kit smiled for the first time. "Rom means something they can't help. It's just the way they are."

"But if you live in Fenton like us, and this is your school, why do you use such funny words? Why don't you talk the same as us?"

Kit smiled again. "Because some words go out of use and new ones are invented, of course. We're finding out about ancient Fenton. For school. We wanted to see what school was like in 1995."

"Wow!" cried Jen. "Do you mean you have a time-machine or something?"

"Oh yes," said Kit. "Every school has. Kids can travel to any century they like and see how people lived. Adults can as well. We always do it at night so the people don't see, but sometimes we make a mistake, like tonight, and somebody *does* see us.

Kids come here all the time. A few steal things—pencils and rulers mostly. Small things we don't have in 2495." He grinned. "I'll tell you a secret, if you promise not to tell anyone else."

"We promise," said Lucy. "Don't we, Jen?" Jen nodded.

"Okay. You know the stories you hear about ghosts and haunted places? Well—there's no such thing as ghosts. What people see is somebody like me, from the future. That's why ghosts are always seen at night, and why they vanish into thin air. Okay?"

That was a relief, thought Lucy. She'd always been scared stiff of ghosts before, but she wouldn't be any more.

"Now gimme headgear," said Kit.

Jen pulled a face. "Not yet. There's millions of things I want to know first."

Kit smiled sadly. "It's dangerous," he said. "For me. If adults came, I would be captured. They would question me to find out about the future, and perform experiments on me too. They would never let me return to my own time."

"Oh, they would!" cried Lucy. "They couldn't be so cruel."

Kit smiled again. "You are wrong," he said. "Think of the cruel things people do to animals."

"No adults are going to come," Jen said. "Not until morning. Won't you stay just half an hour and talk?"

Kit shook his head. "I'd like to," he said. "I'd like to still be here in the morning so I could see the birds. We don't have birds."

"You don't have birds?" gasped Lucy. "Why not?"

Kit looked sheepish. "Well, really I shouldn't have told you that. It's against the rules. What happened was, people put stuff on the land to kill insects—chemical stuff—and it killed all the birds as well. And then the chemicals got washed to the sea and most of the fish died too."

"When did they do that?" asked Jen.

"They're doing it now," Kit replied. "They've been doing it for a long time, and they'll go on doing it."

"What if we tell everybody about the birds and fish?"

Kit laughed. "They won't listen. People do tell them, but they don't listen. They never will. Gimme headgear now." He held out his hands. "Please."

There was a crash outside, then a voice saying, "There's a light on over there." Then another voice, much louder, called out, "Lucy—are you in there, Lucy?"

Lucy gasped. "It's my dad," she hissed. "Quick, Jen—the helmet."

At the sound of the crash, Kit had darted toward the chair. He had almost reached it when Jen made a grab for it, intending to hand the helmet to him. As they collided the chair fell over and the helmet rolled across the floor. Lucy's father strode through the doorway, almost fell over it, and kicked it aside.

"Why has it taken you so long?" he panted. "We've been worried sick."

Now Jen's father appeared in the doorway as well, followed by Mrs. Berry. Jen and Kit scrambled to their feet. The boy backed off, staring at where the helmet lay in a corner by the door. Mrs. Berry looked at him and frowned.

"I don't know who *he* is," she said. "He's not from this school."

"He's Kit. He's—not from around here," said Jen.

"We were talking," said Lucy. "We forgot the time."

"But who is he?" said Mrs. Berry grimly. "That's what I'd like to know."

Jen's father looked at her. "Check around to see

if anything's missing," he said. "If there is, we'll call the police."

"No, Dad!" Jen ran to her father and clung to his arm. "Don't call the police. Awful things will happen to him if you do. He's not a thief—honestly."

"Then what's he doing here at this time of night?" Lucy's father demanded. "And for that matter, why are you and Jennifer still here, Lucy? It shouldn't have taken all this time just to collect a leotard."

"Oh no you don't," Jen's father said as Kit suddenly made a dash toward the door and tried to stop him.

Jen scooped up the helmet as Kit swerved to avoid her father's outstretched arm. "Here!" She tossed it to him and he was gone—through the

doorway and out across the hall, with Lucy's father, Jen's father, and Mrs. Berry charging after him.

He swerved toward the classroom and cried out as Lucy's father loomed in front of him. He swerved again and ran, with the helmet tucked under his arm. As the three adults closed in on him, Kit made one last desperate swerve, burst open the classroom door and plunged into the gloom inside.

Lucy's father reached the classroom first and promptly switched on the lights. Then he glanced around. His mouth fell open. He shook his head and rubbed his eyes. Mrs. Berry and Jen's father gazed over his shoulders into the empty room.

"But he can't just have vanished!" exclaimed Jen's father.

Lucy and Jen had caught up with them now.

"Oh, but he could," said Lucy. "You see—really he's a sort of ghost, isn't he, Jen?"

"Oh, yes," agreed Jen happily. "They all are."

THE HEADLESS RIDER

Grace Hallworth

A long way from the city there was a village that was said to be haunted by a creature so fearsome that anyone who saw it was struck dumb.

The villagers huddled inside their houses at night and even when the doors were bolted and the windows barred they did not feel safe. When they woke one morning and found several of their animals mauled about their necks, the villagers panicked.

They marched to the police station to make a complaint and demand action. One of the villagers had lost a thoroughbred horse and two bulls, and his blood was up. He appointed himself leader of the protest and spokesman, "Matter's gone too far now," he said when they met the policeman. "It's high time that you police went out and worked for your pay instead of hiding in here behind bars like prisoners. If you can't stop this creature then the Commissioner will have to find somebody who can."

But the two policemen were local lads and determined to keep their distance from the creature. "If you don't trouble jumbie, jumbie won't trouble you," replied one of the policemen. And they refused to set foot outside the station after dark.

Soon word reached the Commissioner's ears that the two policemen were not patrolling the village at night because of their fear of the jumbie. "It's a load of mumbo jumbo and hocus-pocus," exploded the Commissioner. "I will not have my rules broken by two cowardly and superstitious policemen." And he immediately sent one of his best corporals to take charge of the village station. No sooner had the corporal arrived and begun his nightly patrol than he was rushed back to the city to the hospital. A villager had found him wandering in the fields early one morning. His mind was in such a state of confusion that he could neither remember who he was nor where he was.

Policeman after policeman came and went in swift succession. They arrived hale and hearty and ready to tackle the jumbie but their stay was short, and in the village the rumor was rife that each policeman was driven mad after a night patrol.

Meanwhile in the city, the Commissioner addressed his men, "What kind of a police force is this?" he asked. "It seems that we have here a nest of mice instead of a team of well-trained men. I shall have to go to the village and settle the matter myself." At these words a young policeman called Dookie spoke: "Sir," he said. "I believe that someone in the village is making monkeys of us. Let me go and prove to the villagers that this so-called jumbie is just flesh and blood like the rest of us." Dookie was an ambitious young man, eager for honors and promotion.

Shortly after Dookie arrived in the village, Mr. Harris, the wealthiest farmer in the district, visited him. He was a big man with a great deal of hair all over his body. When he walked, his massive head hung down as though it were too heavy for the long neck. The strangest thing about him were his knees and the palms of his hands. The skin on them had been scraped away leaving the soft fleshy portions red and raw.

Mr. Harris spoke about many things and as he was about to leave he said, "Now, Constable

Dookie, let me give you a piece of advice. We have a jumbie in this village that don't like policemen, so if I were you I would stay indoors at night."

"True, Mr. Harris?" replied the constable. "Well, let *me* tell you something. Just in case you meet this jumbie of yours, you tell it that Dookie ain't like the other policemen. Tell it from me that the spirit that could frighten me ain't dead yet."

Mr. Harris shook his head and said, "You're a young man, Constable, and you have much to learn. Remember, what ain't meet you ain't pass you." And with that warning he took his leave.

After the meeting, Constable Dookie was determined to prove that he was in command. Every night, as bold as brass, he rode his horse

around the empty village and he met not a soul, neither living nor dead. Sometimes to liven things up he shouted,

Jumbie, jumbie where you hiding?
I am Dookie. I'll be riding every night.
So jumbie, jumbie come and fight.

Soon the children began to chant Dookie's challenge in the playground.

Jumbie, jumbie where you hiding?
I am Dookie. I'll be riding every night.
So jumbie, jumbie come and fight.

It wasn't long before everyone in the village knew it well. And not at all surprising that the calypsonians found a catchy tune to put to the words:

Jumbie, jumbie where you hiding?
I am Dookie and I'll be riding
Every night, every night, every night.
So jumbie, jumbie come and fight.

Of course no self-respecting jumbie would put up with this kind of ridicule for long. And besides, Dookie used to shout his challenge right outside Mr. Harris's house.

One night when Dookie was out on patrol he heard the sound of hooves coming in his direction.

"Strange!" he said to himself. "I have been here for three months and never met another person out at night." He was curious to see who it was that dared to break the self-imposed curfew of the villagers.

As the sound of hooves drew nearer, Dookie's horse began to act very strangely. It became restless, straining to turn around away from whatever was coming. While Dookie was trying to control the horse, he heard something else that set his heart pounding. It was the clanking of chains, clatank! clatank! against the surface of the road. Now, the horse was frantic. It was plunging and snorting so wildly that Dookie could barely stay in the saddle. He was about to give it its head when he saw coming toward him, a gigantic black horse dragging heavy chains. Seated astride the horse was a body without a head. From deep within the belly of the horse came awful groans as though it were in great anguish.

Dookie opened his mouth to scream but not a sound escaped. Fear froze him to his horse and he sat like a carved figure. It was just as well that the horse knew the way home and needed no guidance. It turned and bolted and never stopped until it arrived at the police station. Were it not for the stamping and snorting of the horse, Dookie's

colleagues would not have known that he had arrived; for he could not move or speak and was in a deep coma. The two policemen had to lift him down from his horse and carry him into the station.

It was a full two weeks before Dookie was able to speak and relate what had happened that night. The first thing he did was to write a letter to the Commissioner of Police begging for a transfer back to the city at once.

LOOKING FOR A GHOST

Margaret Mahy

Running along the footpath, fire in his feet, came Sammy Scarlet. He ran on his toes, leaping as he ran, so that he seemed to dance and spin through the twilight like a gray, tumbling bird learning to fly. Sammy leaped as he ran to keep himself brave. He was going to a haunted house. That evening he was going to see a ghost for the first time in his life.

The haunted house was along a city street. It was the last house left in the street, falling to pieces in the middle of a garden of weeds. The glass in the windows was broken, and some of them were crossed over with boards. There was a tall fence around it, but in some places the fence was tumbling down.

"They'll put a bulldozer through that old place soon," said the man in the shop at the corner.

"That's a valuable section, a commercial section."

"Haunted?" Sammy had asked.

"They say there's a ghost, but it only comes out in the evening after the shops have shut up and most people have gone home. I've never seen it," said the man in the corner shop, "and I'm not hanging around here after five-thirty just to watch some ghost. Only a little one too, they say."

"A twilight ghost," Sammy said to himself, and felt as if something breathed cold on the back of his neck and whispered with cold lips in his ear.

Now he ran swiftly through the early evening. Sammy had chosen his time carefully . . . not so dark that his mother would worry about him, not too light for a small, cold ghost.

"Just a quick prowl around!" thought Sammy, as he ran and leaped to keep away the fear that ran beside him like a chilly, pale-eyed dog.

"If I go back now, I'm a coward," thought Sammy, and leaped again. "I've promised myself to see a ghost and I'm *going* to see a ghost."

He knew the street well, but evening changed it. It took him by surprise, seeming to have grown longer and emptier. And at the end of the street the haunted house was waiting. Sammy could see its gate and its tired tumbledown fence. By the gate something moved softly. Sammy leaped in his running, matching his jump to the jump of his heart. But the shadow by the gate was only a little girl bouncing a ball with a stick. She looked up as Sammy came running toward her.

"Hello," she said. "I thought no one ever came here in the evening."

"I've come," Sammy answered, panting. "I'm going to see the ghost."

The little girl looked at him with shadowy black eyes. "A real ghost?" she asked. "What ghost?"

"A ghost that haunts this house," Sammy replied. He was glad of someone to talk to, even a girl with a striped rubber ball in one hand and a stick in the other. She looked back at the house.

"Is this house haunted?" she asked again. "I suppose it looks a bit haunted. It's got cobwebs on it, and thistles in the garden. Aren't you frightened of the ghost, then?"

"I'm not scared of ghosts," said Sammy cheerfully. (He hoped it sounded cheerful.) "They can be pretty scary to some people but, I don't know how

it is, somehow they don't scare me. I'm going through the fence to take a look. They say it is only a little one."

"Why don't you try the gate?" suggested the girl, pushing at the gate with her stick. It creaked open. Sammy stared.

"That's funny," he said. "I looked at the gate earlier and it was locked."

"I'll come with you," said the girl. "My name is Belinda, and I would like to see a ghost too."

"I don't think you'd better," replied Sammy, frowning, "because ghosts can be pretty horrible, you know . . . with sharp teeth and claws and cackling laughs. Bony too!"

"There's nothing wrong with being bony," said Belinda.

She was very thin with a pale, serious face and long brown hair. Though she did not smile she looked friendly and interested. Her heavy shoes made her legs look even thinner, and her dress was

too big for her, Sammy thought. Certainly it was too long, giving her an old-fashioned look.

"If it's scary to be bony," said Belinda, "I might frighten the ghost. Anyway the gate is open and I can go in if I want to." She stepped into the old garden and Sammy stepped after her, half-cross because she was coming into his private adventure, half-pleased to have company. As he came through the gate Sammy felt a cold breath fall on the back of his neck. Turning around slowly he saw nothing. Perhaps it was just a little cool wind sliding into the empty garden with them.

"A garden of thistledown and dandelions," Belinda cried. "A garden all for birds and beetles and ghosts." She seemed to like what she saw. "The lawn is almost as tall as my shoulder. A ghost could easily be in that long grass and just rise up beside us like smoke."

Sammy glanced thoughtfully at the grass, half expecting a smoky shape to billow up and wave its arms at him. But—no smoke, no sound. It was all very still. He could hear cars out on the main road, but they seemed like thin dreams of sound, tiny flies buzzing far away. He walked up the brick path and stood on the front steps of the haunted house, looking at its sad veranda. One of the carved posts was crumbling down and the veranda sagged with it.

"You'd feel cruel just standing on this veranda," Sammy remarked. "It looks so limp and sick."

"Cruelty to verandas!" said Belinda seriously. "Stand on it lightly, Sammy, and we'll go inside. I think a ghost would be more likely to be inside, don't you?"

"The door will be locked, won't it?" Sammy said. Then, "How did you know my name?" he asked, looking puzzled.

"You *look* like a Sammy," was all she said. She pushed the door and it slowly opened, like a black mouth opening to suck them into its shadows.

"I might stay out here," Sammy said. "The floor could cave in or something." His voice was quiet and squashed small by the heavy silence of the whole house and garden.

"You don't have to be afraid," Belinda told him kindly. "It's just an old, empty house, and old houses were made of good wood." Through the dark door she slid and vanished. Sammy *had* to follow her. Then he got the most terrible fright. He was standing in a hall so dim and dusty that he could see almost nothing. But what he *could* see was a dim and dusty figure at the other end of the hall moving slowly toward him.

"The ghost!" cried Sammy.

Belinda looked back at him. He could not see her face properly, but for some reason he thought she might be smiling.

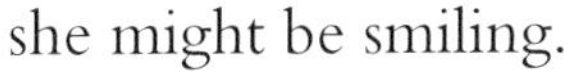

"It isn't a ghost," she told him. "It's a looking-glass. There's a tall cupboard at the end with a looking glass in its door. It's your own reflection that's frightening you."

Sammy blinked and saw that what she said could be true. They walked cautiously up the hall. The looking glass reflected the open doorway behind them. It was so dark inside that the evening outside looked bright and pearly.

Sammy rubbed his finger across the looking-glass.

The looking glass moved and they heard a low moaning.

"The ghost!" gasped Sammy again, but it was just the cupboard door. It was a little bit open and creaking when Sammy touched it.

"Come upstairs!" Belinda said. "They were nice, once, these stairs. They used to be polished every day."

"How can you tell?" asked Sammy, looking up the dark stairway.

"They are smooth under the dust," Belinda replied, "smooth with feet walking, and hands polishing. But that was a long time ago."

"How can you see your way upstairs?" Sammy asked. "It's so dark."

"There's enough light," she answered, already several steps above him. Sammy came after her. Out of the dark came a hand, soft and silent as the shadows, and laid silken fingers across his face.

"The ghost!" cried Sammy for the third time.

"Cobwebs, only cobwebs!" called Belinda back to him. Sammy touched his face. His own fingers, stiff with fright, found only cobwebs, just as Belinda had said. He stumbled and scrambled up after her onto the landing. There was a window boarded over. It was easy to peep through the cracks and look over the thistly garden and down the empty street.

"There used to be grass there," Belinda whispered, peering out. "Grass and cows. But that was a long time ago." She straightened up. "Come through *this* door," she said in her ordinary voice.

Sammy did not want to be left behind. They went through the door into a small room. The boards had partly slipped away from the windows. Evening light brightened the walls and striped the ceiling. There were the remains of green curtains and a rocking chair with one rocker broken. Sitting in the chair was a very old doll. It looked as if someone had put it down and had gone out to play for a moment. The doll seemed to expect someone to be back to play with it. Sammy looked over to the doll and around the room, and then out through the window. "There's no ghost," he said, "and it's getting late. I'll have to be going."

The ghost did not seem as important as it had a moment ago, but Sammy thought he would remember the silent, tumbling house and its wild garden, long after he had stopped thinking about ghosts.

They went down the stairs again and Sammy did not jump at the cobwebs. They went past the looking glass and he creaked the cupboard door on purpose this time. Now the sound did not frighten him. It was gentle and complaining, not fierce or angry.

"It only wants to be left alone," Belinda said, and that was what it sounded like.

They walked down the hall and Sammy turned to wave goodbye to his reflection before he shut the door. The reflection waved back at him from the end of a long tunnel of shadow. Outside, the evening darkened. Stars were showing.

"No ghost!" said Sammy, shaking his head.

They walked to the gate.

"Will you be coming back some other night to look for the ghost?" Belinda asked.

"I don't think so," Sammy answered. "I don't really believe in ghosts. I just thought there might be one. I've looked once and there isn't one and that's enough."

He turned to run off home, but something made him stop and look sharply at Belinda.

"Did you see *your* reflection in that looking glass?" he asked curiously. "I don't remember your reflection."

Belinda did not answer his question. Instead she asked him one of her own.

"Everyone has a reflection, don't they?" It was hard to see her in the late evening, but once again Sammy thought she might be smiling.

"You went up the stairs first," he went on. "Why didn't you brush the cobwebs away?"

"I'm not as tall as you," Belinda said.

Sammy peered at her, waiting for her to say something more. Just for a moment, very faintly, he felt that chilly breeze touch the back of his neck again.

"No ghost!" he said at last. "No such things as ghosts!" Then, without a goodbye, he ran off home, rockets in the heels of his shoes.

Belinda watched him go.

"The question is," she said to herself, "whether he would recognize a ghost, supposing he saw one."

She went back through the gate and locked it carefully after her. She was already faint and far off in the evening, and as she pushed the bolt home she disappeared entirely.

THE TINKER AND THE GHOST

A Spanish folktale retold by
Ralph Steele Boggs and Mary Gould Davis

On the wide plain not far from the city of Toledo, there once stood a great gray castle. For many years before this story begins, no one had dwelt there, because the castle was haunted. There was no living soul within its walls, and yet at night, a thin, sad voice moaned and wept and wailed through the huge, empty rooms. And on All Hallows' Eve, a ghostly light appeared in the chimney, a light that flared and died and flared again against the dark sky.

Learned doctors and brave adventurers had come to the castle on All Hallows' Eve and tried to exorcise the ghost. Each one had been found the next morning in the great hall of the castle, sitting lifeless before the empty fireplace.

Now one day in late October there came to the little village that nestled around the castle walls a brave and jolly tinker whose name was Esteban. And while he sat in the marketplace, mending the pots and pans, the good wives told him about the haunted castle. It was All Hallows' Eve, they said, and if he would wait until nightfall he could see the strange, ghostly light flare up from the chimney. He might, if he dared go near enough, hear the thin, sad voice echo through the silent rooms.

"If I dare!" Esteban repeated scornfully. "You must know, good wives, that I—Esteban—fear nothing, neither ghost nor human. I will gladly sleep in the castle tonight and keep this dismal spirit company."

The good wives looked at him in amazement. Did Esteban know that if he succeeded in banishing the ghost the owner of the castle would give him a thousand gold *reales*?

Esteban chuckled. If that was how matters stood, he would certainly go to the castle at nightfall and do his best to get rid of the thing that haunted it. But he was a man who liked plenty to eat and drink and a fire to keep him company. They must bring to him a load of firewood, a side of bacon, a flask of wine, a dozen fresh eggs, and a frying pan. This the good wives gladly did. And as the dusk fell, Esteban loaded these things onto his donkey's back and set out for the castle. And you may be very sure that not one of the village people went very far along the way with him!

It was a dark night with a chill wind blowing and a hint of rain in the air. Esteban unsaddled his donkey and set him to graze on the short grass of the deserted courtyard. Then he carried his food and his firewood into the great hall. It was dark as pitch there. Bats beat their soft wings in his face, and the air felt cold and musty. He lost no time in piling some of his firewood in one corner of the huge stone fireplace and in lighting it. As the red and golden flames leaped up the chimney, Esteban rubbed his hands. Then he settled himself comfortably on the hearth.

"*That* is the thing to keep off both cold and fear," he said.

Carefully slicing some bacon, he laid it in the pan and set it over the flames. How good it smelled! And how cheerful the sound of its crisp sizzling!

He had just lifted his flask to take a deep drink of the good wine when down the chimney there came a voice—a thin, sad voice. "*Oh, me!*" it wailed. "*Oh, me! Oh, me!*"

Esteban swallowed the wine and set the flask carefully down beside him.

"Not a very cheerful greeting, my friend," he said, as he moved the bacon on the pan so that it should be equally brown in all its parts. "But bearable to a man who is used to the braying of his donkey."

"*Oh, me!*" sobbed the voice. "*Oh, me! Oh, me!*"

Esteban lifted the bacon carefully from the hot fat and laid it on a bit of brown paper to drain. Then he broke an egg into the frying pan. As he gently shook the pan so that the edges of his egg should be crisp and brown and the yolk soft, the voice came again. Only this time it was shrill and frightened.

"*Look out below,*" it called. "*I'm falling!*"

"All right," answered Esteban, "only don't fall into the frying pan."

With that there was a thump, and there on the hearth lay a man's leg! It was a good enough leg, and it was clothed in half of a pair of brown corduroy trousers.

Esteban ate his egg and a piece of bacon and drank again from the flask of wine. The wind howled around the castle, and the rain beat against the windows.

Then, "*Look out below,*" called the voice sharply. "*I'm falling!*"

There was a thump, and on the hearth there lay a second leg, just like the first!

Esteban moved it away from the fire and piled on more wood. Then he warmed the fat in the frying pan and broke into it a second egg.

"*Look out below!*" roared the voice. And now it was no longer thin, but strong and lusty. "*Look out below! I'm falling!*"

"Fall away," Esteban answered cheerfully. "Only don't spill my egg."

There was a thump, heavier than the first two, and on the hearth there lay a trunk. It was clothed in a blue shirt and a brown corduroy coat.

Esteban was eating his third egg and the last of the cooked bacon when the voice called again, and down fell first one arm and then the other.

Now, thought Esteban, as he put the frying pan on the fire and began to cook more bacon. *Now there is only the head left to fall. I confess that I am rather curious to see the head.*

"LOOK OUT BELOW!" thundered the voice. "I'M FALLING—FALLING!"

And down the chimney there came tumbling a head!

It was a good enough head, with thick black hair, a long black beard, and dark eyes that looked a little strained and anxious. Esteban's bacon was

only half-cooked. Nevertheless, he removed the pan from the fire and laid it on the hearth. And it is a good thing that he did, because before his eyes the parts of the body joined together, and a living man—or his ghost—stood before him! And *that* was a sight that might have startled Esteban into burning his fingers with the bacon fat.

"Good evening," said Esteban. "Will you have an egg and a bit of bacon?"

"No, I want no food," the ghost answered. "But I will tell you this, right here and now. You are the only man, out of all those who have come to the castle, to stay here until I could get my body together again. The others died of sheer fright before I was half-finished."

"That is because they did not have sense enough to bring food and fire with them," Esteban replied coolly. And he turned back to his frying pan.

"Wait a minute!" pleaded the ghost. "If you will help me a bit more, you will save my soul and get me into the kingdom of heaven. Out in the courtyard, under a cypress tree, there are buried three bags—one of copper coins, one of silver coins, and one of gold coins. I stole them from some thieves and brought them here to the castle to hide. No sooner did I have them buried than the thieves overtook me, murdered me, and cut my body into pieces. But they did not find the coins. Now you come with me and dig them up. Give the copper coins to the church, the silver coins to the poor, and keep the gold coins for yourself. Then I will have expiated my sins and can go to the kingdom of heaven."

This suited Esteban. So he went out into the courtyard with the ghost. And you should have heard how the donkey brayed when he saw them!

When they reached the cypress tree in a corner of the courtyard, the ghost said, "Dig."

"Dig yourself," answered Esteban.

So the ghost dug, and after a time the three bags of money appeared.

"Now will you promise to do just what I asked you to do?" said the ghost.

"Yes, I promise," Esteban answered.

"Then," said the ghost, "strip my garments from me."

This Esteban did, and instantly the ghost disappeared, leaving his clothes lying there on the short grass of the courtyard. It went straight up to heaven and knocked on the gate. Saint Peter opened it and, when the spirit explained that he had expiated his sins, gave him a cordial welcome.

Esteban carried the coins into the great hall of the castle, fried and ate another egg, and then went peacefully to sleep before the fire.

The next morning when the village people came to carry away Esteban's body, they found him making an omelet out of the last of the fresh eggs.

"Are you alive?" they gasped.

"I am," Esteban answered. "And the food and the firewood lasted through the night very nicely. Now I will go to the owner of the castle and collect my thousand gold *reales*. The ghost has gone for good and all. You will find his clothes lying out in the courtyard."

And before their astonished eyes he loaded the bags of coins on the donkey's back and departed.

First he collected the thousand gold *reales* from the grateful lord of the castle. Then he returned to Toledo, gave the copper coins to his parish priest, and faithfully distributed the silver ones among the poor. And on the thousand *reales* and the golden coins he lived in idleness and a great contentment for many years.

PONKYFOOT

David Parker

There was once a terrible pirate called Ponkyfoot. Ponkyfoot was the most dangerous pirate who ever was, and whenever another pirate heard his name his face would turn as white as his toenails and his hands would flutter in the breeze. Ponkyfoot was called Ponky for short.

From a distance Ponky looked a bit like a barrel of tar with a red scarf wound around the top. Just below the scarf, his black eyebrows twitched like crabs' nippers and his black eyes bulged like cannonballs and his angry face was as red as boiling tomatoes.

But the very worst thing about Ponkyfoot was his left leg, which was short and thick. It was made from an old ship's timber and it ended in a peg. So that wherever Ponkyfoot walked the leg made a noise so horrible, it would turn your blood to seawater. Ponk! Ponk! Ponk! it went, and everyone else's feet would shake in their boots like jellyfish.

In the harbor below the town lay Ponkyfoot's ship, the bad ship *Thunderbone.*

One night when there was no moon and the stars were covered with clouds and the water was dark and cold as death, Ponkyfoot decided to put to sea.

"I'll hunt a fine ship and blow her to pieces and leave her sailors in the sea," he thought, "or if there aren't any fine ships to fire at I'll battle with one of me pirate enemies and sink *his* bones to the bottom." And he smiled a horrible smile.

Ponkyfoot looked down fiercely on his scowling pirate crew, standing before him on the fiery deck of *Thunderbone*. There stood Ironhead, his huge hand on a cutlass with a blade as wide as a plank. A scar ran from his nose to his ear and his bald head shone like oil. At the wheel was the grim pirate known as Oyster, saying nothing. He opened his mouth only to eat. Not far from him was a strange figure with a gag in his mouth, jumping up and down. His name was Manywords and he was greatly feared by the other men because he drove them mad with endless talk that no one could understand. Behind the group of frightful men on the deck was perhaps the worst of them all, the great round shape of the evil pirate cook, Glob. These, and the rest of Ponkyfoot's angry crew, stood waiting for their captain's order to sail, as the cold wind cut into their cruel faces.

Ponkyfoot looked over the side, down into the black water flowing past his ship. The tide was beginning to turn. He lifted his head and shouted a command and the strong wind carried his voice like a scrap of paper. The pirates ran over the deck at once. Some of them laid hold of the capstan and others climbed the rigging. Oyster stood ready at the wheel and Glob disappeared below like a squid sliding into a hole. As they worked at their evil ship they sang a terrible song:

Thunder and smoke and blood and bone—
Away, boys, together!
Fear no dead men, cold as stone—
Never, boys, never!

Slowly, the sails filled, and the anchor came dripping out of the sea. Oyster spun the great wheel and *Thunderbone* moved silently out of the harbor and began to rise and fall to the long sea

swell. Soon there was no sound on deck but the creaking of spars and ropes and the crash of the sea as the pirate ship lifted and plunged her head like a salty horse. Oyster stood silent as stone at the wheel, gripping its wooden spokes with his thick fingers and looking out into the darkness.

Ponkyfoot paced the deck. Now and then he would clamp his long brass telescope to his eye, looking for signs of a ship he could chase and fight and plunder. But he could see nothing except the gray sea and the white, broken waves. He became angry.

"It's time I found a ship," he growled. "I want gold and dead men's bones." Ponky turned to face his crew. "We want gold and dead men's bones, don't we lads?" he roared. A fierce shout rose from the men on the deck. Ironhead began to call out a chorus in the howling wind and every pirate on deck lifted his head and joined in the terrible song.

Bones of ships and bones of men shining in the sun,
Aye! Give us blood and give us gold and give us
Spanish rum!

At that moment, Ponkyfoot heard the sound of a great bell. He saw every one of his pirate crew go stiff with fright. At once the sea was covered with fog. The wind dropped, until there was only the noise of the rocking ship. Then the sound of the bell came again. Every sailor peered out into the fog. Ponkyfoot swung his telescope from one side to another, but he could see nothing, only the swirling mist and the water lying at the sides of the ship. The bell sounded again with a great clang.

"It's the ghost ship," they began to mutter to one another, "the ship no sailor has ever seen and lived to speak of." Whoever saw the ghost ship would join her crew, old sailormen used to say.

Ponky's heart started to bang, his sword shook in his belt and his pipe went out at once. His hands gripped the rails of his ship and his eyes turned toward the place in the fog from which the sound had come. Still he could see nothing. Once again the bell sounded across the water, and Ponkyfoot and his pirate crew saw through the cold mist the form of a ship moving silently toward them.

Ponky and his pirates stood quite still on the deck of *Thunderbone*, staring in fear as the ghost ship came nearer. In perfect silence it came closer until it drew alongside *Thunderbone*. At last Ponkyfoot saw its crew.

"They're skeletons!" Ponky whispered. "The bones of dead sailormen!"

White and stiff the sailors of the ghost ship stood upon the deck, and a skeleton held the wheel. Within a moment, the terrible ship sailed by, the mist closed around her, and she was gone.

At that very moment a bell sounded with a loud

"Bong!" Ponkyfoot opened his mouth wide to shout in fear but no sound would come. He gripped the ship's rail and stared out at the gray water. He saw only a great bell rolling in the sea mist, nodding its head like a sleepy old man. A sea bird rode on its top, rolling from side to side in the green waves.

"We've seen enough, lads!" Ponky shouted to his pirate crew. "We've seen the ghost ship, that carries off dead sailormen. We'll chase and fight no more. We'll go about and drive for home lads! Let her run before the wind, away from mist and bones and the ghost ship come to take us."

Soon the shining black ship turned and began to cut through the sharp, cold waves. Her sails banged and stretched, and *Thunderbone* ran hard toward the sun at the edge of the sea.

But Ponkyfoot and his pirate crew and the bad ship *Thunderbone* were never seen again—not at sea, and not in the harbor. Some people say Ponky has sailed to an island no one has ever seen. But old sailormen talk instead of the ghost ship that carries off dead men. When the sea is wild and the wind is loud and running through the town, *then* you'll hear old Ponky's ghost, they say. When the night is black and full of storm you'll hear his wooden leg. Ponk! Ponk! Ponk! it goes, ringing through the streets. And doors and windows slam and bang and the town goes straight to bed.

HANS AND HIS MASTER

Ruth Manning-Sanders

There was once a rich old gentleman who was no better than he should be, and he died and was buried in the family vault. But that wasn't the end of him. Every night his ghost came up into the house and made such an uproar that no one could sleep: he stamped here, he clattered there; he rattled and banged and flung things about, till all the household were nigh crazy with terror.

The gracious lady, his widow, was grieved at heart. And one day, when she had gone down into the kitchen, she said, "Ah, why cannot my late husband find rest, so that you and I, my poor servants, might have at least a little peace?"

Well now, sitting in the kitchen, drinking his soup, was old Hans, the coachman. And he spoke up and said, "If the gracious lady will leave the matter to me, I think I know of a remedy. But for a couple of days I must have a hundred gold pieces, and also a coffin. I will lay me down in the coffin; and if the gracious lady will have me carried into the vault, coffin and all, and set alongside of my master, I will soon find out why my poor master can't rest in his grave."

Now Hans was the oldest servant of the house, and his lady liked and trusted him. So she gave him the hundred gold pieces and ordered a coffin to be made for him. And while the coffin was in the making, Hans took the gold pieces and buried them in the stable. Then, when the coffin was ready, Hans got into it, stretched himself out, and bade them put on the lid. And that they did, and carried the coffin down to the vault, and laid it beside the coffin of the master.

And Hans lay quiet in his coffin through the day and through the evening, until the great clock in the stable yard struck midnight.

And as the last stroke of the clock died away, Hans heard the lid of his master's coffin burst open; so he immediately banged up the lid of his own coffin likewise. Then the master sat up in *his* coffin, and Hans sat up in his coffin. Then the master climbed out of his coffin, and so did Hans.

There they stood, master and man, looking at one another.

"Hans, Hans," said the master, "how came you here?"

"Exactly as you did, gracious master," said Hans. "I am dead and buried, and waiting humbly to serve you as I did in life."

"And where are you going now, Hans?"

"Exactly where you are going, gracious master, humbly to serve you."

"But I am going up to the house, Hans, for I have still something to see to."

"That I have also, gracious master, and just for that reason I can find no rest in my coffin."

"But what in the world can you have to see about, Hans?"

"It's this way, gracious master (humbly to serve you); I had a little sum of money put by and I buried it in the stable. Now I must just go and have a look, for I fear that thieves may have taken it."

"I too have a fear on my mind, Hans. So come, we will go together."

So the master led the way to the door of the vault, and Hans followed. And when they reached that door, the master slipped through the keyhole.

"Come along, Hans," said he.

"Ah, good master—humbly to serve you—I can't come, the keyhole is too narrow."

Then the master put his hand on the lock of the door; the door sprang open, and Hans stepped through. But the master shook his head and said, "Hans, Hans, what is this? I fear you are not dead!"

"Not dead, gracious master? Most certainly I am dead! But the manner of the flesh still clings about me, and I have yet to learn the way of ghosts."

"That may be, Hans—but it is strange."

"Don't shake your gracious head, master; I shall soon learn."

"That may be, Hans," said the master again. And they crossed the courtyard together. And when they came to the door of the house, the master chuckled and said, "First let us go through the rooms and frighten the women."

And he led the way to the kitchen.

And there again he slipped through the keyhole. But again he had to open the door before Hans could follow him.

"Oh Hans, Hans," said he, "this is very strange! I fear you are not dead after all!"

"Not dead, master—humbly to serve you! Didn't you see me get out of my coffin? A coffin is made for the dead, not for the living. But the hours of my death are short, and the hours of my life long, and the ways of the living are not cast aside in a moment."

"Well, now to work," said the master. And he went to the cupboard, snatched down one thing after the other, and flung everything on the floor. And what he saw his master doing, Hans did likewise: pots, dishes, plates, cups and saucers, knives and forks went flying; chairs and tables were overturned. The racket they made woke the whole household; the master chuckled and chuckled; Hans roared with laughter. But the strange thing was that whatever the master overturned put itself right again, and the things he threw from the cupboard bounced up and set themselves in their proper place, sound and whole; whereas what Hans threw down was smashed into a thousand pieces, and the pieces remained strewed about the floor.

Then the master shook his head once more, and said, "Hans, Hans, my mind misgives me. I fear you are not dead!"

"Not dead, gracious master, not dead, how can that be, and me laid in my coffin? It is only that my life is not yet far distant, and so my hand is still heavy. I was never quick like you to learn new ways. Give me but a little time, and my hand will be as light as yours."

"Maybe, maybe," said the master. "But come, the night passes. Let us get on with the game."

And he led Hans from room to room, snatched the pictures from the walls, overturned the furniture, and threw everything pell-mell, making such an uproar that the people in the house put their fingers in their ears, drew the bedclothes over their heads, and lay quaking in sheer terror.

"Now," said the master at last, "I think they are scared enough, so we will go down to the cellar."

And down to the cellar he went, and Hans followed.

The master wasn't chuckling any more, he was sighing and groaning. "Hans," said he, "I will show you my trouble."

He laid his hand on a huge cask, and the cask moved from its place as lightly as a bubble; and

there, underneath it, a hole opened in the cellar floor, and from the hole rose up a huge cauldron full of gold.

"Hans, Hans," groaned the master, "this gold is the cause of my trouble, and because of it my soul can find no rest. It was entrusted to me to bestow upon an orphanage, but I kept it for myself and hid it here. Ah Hans, Hans, if the orphans could but get this gold, then I might have peace. But all in vain I groan and sigh: the orphans can never get it, for no living man knows that it is here. So here it must remain to all eternity; and to all eternity must I sigh and groan, and play the fool—if, by so doing, I may forget my sorrows for a few brief moments."

Then the master waved his hand over the cauldron. It sank once more, and the ground covered it. He touched the cask with his finger, and the cask moved back into its place as lightly as a bubble.

"Now, Hans," sighed the master, "we will see to your affair."

So they went to the stable, and there Hans took a spade, and began to dig in the corner where he had buried his hundred gold pieces.

"Hans," said the master, "why do you dig?"

"To find the gold that I buried, master."

"Oh Hans, Hans, I fear you are not dead! The dead have only to wave a hand and the money will come out by itself."

"Not dead, gracious master—humbly to serve you! Not dead! Most surely I am dead! Did you not see me in my coffin? But I have not yet fully learned how I must go on, and so I dig as I did in life."

Then Hans dug up all his gold and counted it coin by coin.

"Yes," said he, "it is all here. And now I must bury it again."

And he began shoveling back the earth over the gold, slowly and carefully, taking his time.

"Work quicker, work quicker!" cried the master. "For soon the cocks will crow, and then we must lie down in our coffins."

But Hans was not to be hurried, however much his master fretted and fumed. However, at last he filled in the earth over his gold, and patted the earth smooth, and laid down his spade.

Cock-a-doodle-do! Faint, hoarse, and sleepy, a cock crowed from the poultry yard.

"Hans, Hans, did you hear that? The gray cock has crowed! We must hasten to our coffins!"

"I will come, gracious master—humbly to serve you. I will come very soon. But first I am going back up into the house to frighten the people just a little bit more. For that is great fun, gracious master, and to remember it will make me laugh when I have to lie down in my coffin."

And Hans ran up into the house and began to throw things about, making all the noise he could. But the master stood at the house door, wringing his hands.

Cock-a-doodle-doo-oo! Out in the poultry house there came a glimmer of dawn light. A cock stirred on his perch and crowed between sleep and waking.

"Hans, Hans, did you hear that? The red cock has crowed! If you don't come at once I shall leave you and go alone, for it is time we were back in our coffins!"

Now Hans wished for nothing better than that his master should go and leave him, so he flung a few dishes from the dresser and shouted, "I come

directly, gracious master, I come directly! But first a little more fun!"

Cock-a-doodle-doo! Cock-a-doodle-doo! Cock-a-doodle-doo! The rising sun darted a ray of light up from behind the courtyard wall; the ray flashed through the window of the poultry house, and three cocks crowed clear and loud.

"Hans, Hans, the gray cock has crowed, the red cock has crowed, the white cock has crowed, and the dawn has come!" The wailing voice of the master grew fainter and fainter, and was silent. He had gone back to his coffin in the vault.

Now the house was very quiet. Hans tiptoed up to his mistress's door and called, "Mistress, gracious mistress, wake up!"

"It is easy to wake, Hans, when one has not slept," answered the gracious widowed lady. And she opened her door and came out.

Then Hans told her all that had happened. And she called her servants, and everyone went down to the cellar. There, after much heaving and straining, they managed to move the great cask from its place. And then they took spades and pickaxes and dug and dug, and at last unearthed the cauldron full of gold. They packed the gold into sacks; and even before the mistress sat down to breakfast, she had the sacks of gold carried to the orphanage.

After that the house was put in order. And on the following night, and on every night thereafter, the gracious widowed lady and her servants were able to sleep peacefully in their beds. Never again did the master come to make the night hideous with his uproar. Only, on the first night, Hans waked from his sleep to find the master standing by his bed.

"Hans, Hans," said the master, "I fear you have sadly deceived me! And yet I am grateful to you, my valiant servant, because what you have done was to my greatest good. By your means the wrong has been righted; and now I can go to my rest."

Beezlebub's Baby

Joan Aiken

Aunt Ada came to live with us at the end of the summer holidays. Before, we'd only seen her at Christmas and didn't realize just how awful she was. Now, we had her all the time.

She was tall and pale with a face like a melon and hair done in a gray knob on top of her head. Her eyes were the color of cherrystones. Her skirts came almost to her ankles. And her voice went nonstop.

"Don't you eat that orange in here, miss! Take it in the garden. Let me see those hands, young man. *Just* as I thought. You go straight off and wash them. *What* is that *dog* doing on that bed?"

"Can't you stop her, Mum?" I asked, but Mum said helplessly, "She is your father's elder sister, you see . . ."

Dad, who is a merchant seaman, went to sea for longer and longer trips.

Aunt Ada had Stuart's room, and Stu had to move in with Kev. I was lucky being a girl, I had a room of my own. At least I thought I was lucky . . .

Aunt Ada took over the shopping from Mum, she said that was only fair. What wasn't fair, she expected me to help her, after I got home from school.

Which was why we were coming out of the Dick Turpin shopping mall at half-past five on a cold October afternoon, each carrying two frightfully heavy bags of shopping.

"No use waiting for a bus, love," said a man at the Swilly Valley Service stop. "They're out on strike."

"Disgraceful!" said Aunt Ada, and she carried on and on about the wicked ways of bus drivers.

"We'd better start walking," I said sadly. "It's only a mile and a half."

"We'd best go along the towpath," said Aunt Ada. "That's only half the distance."

"Oh no, don't let's do that," I said in a great hurry.

"Why ever not?" snapped Aunt Ada, staring at me with her cherrystone eyes.

"Because—because it's sure to be muddy."

"Don't be ridiculous, child! It hasn't rained all week. Come along and don't argue. I never *met* such children for argument."

"*Please* don't let's go that way," I said again. Dusk was beginning to thicken along Potter's Road; by the time we got to the canal bridge, it would be quite dark.

"Quiet, miss! I don't want to hear another word. Come along now—step out! Don't show me that sulky face."

And she stomped on ahead, every now and then turning around to glare at me and make sure that I was following.

Well, I thought, she'll see it first. That's one comfort.

Another comfort was that our dog Turk wasn't with us. Turk will never, ever go along that stretch of the towpath; he just turns around and runs home if anyone tries to take him that way, even in broad daylight.

By the time we got to the canal bridge, it was full dark. And I could hear the sound long before we got there.

So could Aunt Ada.

"That's funny," she says. "I can hear a baby crying. Can *you* hear a baby, Janet?"

"Yes," I said glumly, because I could.

"This is *no* time of day for a baby to be out," said Aunt Ada. "Its mother ought to be ashamed of herself! I've a good mind to tell her so."

I didn't think its mother would have bothered much about Aunt Ada's bad opinion even if she had heard it, two hundred years ago.

"Where can that baby be? Can it be under the bridge?" Aunt Ada said.

As we drew near, the streetlights up above shone down on the path and made the blackness under the bridge seem even blacker. And the crying became louder and angrier.

"*I* believe," said Aunt Ada, "*I* believe that somebody's *left* that baby under the bridge. Well—that somebody is going to be in bad, bad trouble!"

And she stepped into the darkness under the bridge. I lagged back, but she called, "Come *on*, Janet!"

Still, I was far enough back so that I could see the baby, all wet and dripping, and with a faint shine about it, like a dead fish that's gone bad, come climbing out of the canal water and run to Aunt Ada.

She dropped both her shopping bags; oranges and yogurt cartons and toilet rolls shot in all directions.

I had expected that Aunt Ada would run off, screaming blue murder. Most people do that, when they see a ghost baby. But not she.

"Why, you poor, poor little mite!" she said. "Who *put* you in the water? Who did such a dreadful thing?"

"It was his mother—" I began to say. "She was a highwayperson two hundred years ago—she was called Beezlebub Bess—"

But Aunt Ada was taking no notice of me. She was cosseting that baby, patting it and clucking over it like a hen that finds a diamond egg in the nesting box.

"*You*'ll have to manage the shopping the rest of

the way, Janet," she says to me. "I have to carry this poor little half-drowned angel."

And she picks up the ghost baby. Angel it certainly was not.

I don't think anyone had ever picked it up before. Mostly they run for their lives. A few have dropped dead on the spot. The baby wasn't at all used to being picked up. It struggled.

"None of that, now!" she said, giving it a smart shake. And to me: "Poor thing, it's as light as a feather. Half-starved, I daresay. Come on, Janet, look sharp, pick up those bags and let's be off. The sooner this little angel is into some dry clothes the better."

"But you can't take it to our home!" I said.

"Why ever not?" She was striding away along the path as fast as her long skirts would allow. She didn't stop to listen to me.

"It's a highwaylady's baby! She dropped it in the canal when the Bow Street runners were chasing her. Her name was Beezlebub Bess!"

Aunt Ada paid no heed; so I didn't go on to tell her that Bess's black horse Jericho had jumped clean over the twenty-foot canal and so helped its mistress escape from the runners. What became of her after that was never known. But the baby that fell into the canal was drowned and had been making a ghostly nuisance of itself ever since on the towpath. Some people call it the Wicked Baby, and not for nothing.

"You can't take it home!" I repeated.

But Aunt Ada did.

"I *really* don't think we can have that baby in the house," said Mum helplessly.

Mum is helpless just when she ought to be firm.

"And what Edward will say I can't imagine," she added.

"Edward won't be home for five months," Aunt Ada said. "And the baby can sleep in Janet's room."

My room! But Aunt Ada went to the United Baptists' Jumble Sale and bought a carrycot for 50 pence.

At night the baby was a real menace. When it wasn't crying, grizzling, or whimpering, it would be out of the cot and fidgeting around the room. Nothing was safe. Books and tapes fell off shelves, bottles and pots rolled off the chest of drawers, clothes were dragged off hangers, and in the middle of the night I'd feel its tiny little ice-cold fingers scrabbling at me or pulling my hair.

How would you like to share your bedroom with a ghost baby?

Turk wouldn't come in my bedroom any more, not even into the house, he stood and growled in the back doorway.

Elsewhere in the house, the baby was just as much of a hazard. One look from it was enough to send the TV into spirals. The lights fused if it crawled across the room; and a chicken that Mum put in to roast came out frozen instead, just because little Beezlebub went and peered in the oven ten minutes before dinnertime.

The boys and I couldn't stand it any longer. We wrote to Dad. He phoned from Cairo and told Aunt Ada that she must find somewhere else to live.

To our amazement this didn't faze her at all.

"I've already thought of that," she told him calmly. "I have applied for sheltered Council accommodation, for me and my little angel. And I am pleased to say that they have put me at the top of the waiting-list."

Another month went by; but we felt we could bear it now, as long as we knew that it wouldn't be forever. We could bear the baby's tearing up the mail in the letterbox, and eating Turk's dinner out of his bowl, turning the washing in the machine bright scarlet, making Mum's cake mix taste as salty as the Sahara. We could bear the neighbors grumbling because it howled all night long, and the gas meter man refusing to call because he got his ankles bitten, and sending huge estimated bills.

We could bear the freezing cold in the house, and fish swimming in the bath.

We could bear it all if we knew the pair were going.

Well, in the end, Aunt Ada did go to her sheltered accommodation. But, guess what? The baby wouldn't stay there. She took it there okay, but it comes right back. It drifts through windows, it slides through keyholes. Night after night, there it is in my room, grizzling, scrabbling, rummaging in my drawers, poking me with its icy little fingers. The neighbors still complain, but what can we do?

It's got fond of us, see.

GABRIEL

Barbee Oliver Carleton

There was an old house on the edge of town belonging to Mr. and Mrs. Gould. Right in the middle of the house there was a little tower. In this little tower lived Gabriel, a small and friendly ghost.

The Goulds had had Gabriel a long time without even knowing it, and Gabriel loved them very much. He spent every minute with them that he could spare from haunting his tower.

So that is how Gabriel knew about birthdays. The mysterious packages hidden under the bed! The secret swishes of tissue paper! The yummy cake and the shining candles and the dishes of ice cream and the splendid paper streamers in the dining room! And, best of all, the boys and girls from town who came tiptoeing in at the back door to make it a surprise!

Twice a year all these wonderful things happened, once for Mrs. Gould and once for Mr. Gould. Just thinking about it made Gabriel go tingly all over, with chills up and down the back and happy shivers in the tummy. Finally he could stand it no longer.

"You know what?" Gabriel said to his friend, Owl, who lived in a tree outside his window. "I'm going to have a birthday!"

"Ghosts," hooted Owl, "don't have birthdays!"

"This one does!" said Gabriel firmly.

"Hmmm," said Owl. "When?"

Gabriel thought very hard. Then he hunted all through the calendar. At last he smiled a faraway smile. "I'll know," said Gabriel, "by the yummy smells in the kitchen and the splendid streamers in the dining room. And the things under the bed. And mostly, I'll know by the children, whispering all over town!"

"Maybe," said Owl.

That was in the summer. As excited as could be, Gabriel waited for his birthday, crossing the days off the calendar one by one. The weeks went by, autumn came and the leaves fell, red and gold. The children piled them high and jumped into them. Mr. Gould raked them over his rose beds. Mrs. Gould finished her fall cleaning.

"Had your birthday yet?" Owl asked Gabriel.

"No-o," said Gabriel, "but I will soon." And he

crossed off another day. "Maybe," thought Gabriel, "it will be tomorrow." But no, there had not been a single swish of tissue paper, not even a smell of chocolate cake. "Maybe they're making it a surprise," thought Gabriel. But no, he had not noticed a thing under the bed. Nowhere around town had there been a whisper or a tiptoe. "Maybe," said Gabriel slowly, "maybe Owl is right. Maybe ghosts DON'T have birthdays!"

This was such a sad thought that Gabriel decided to go away for a while and forget all about birthdays. Nearby there was an old barn that looked as if it needed haunting. There went Gabriel.

But the barn was full of drafts at night, and Gabriel grew homesick for Mr. and Mrs. Gould.

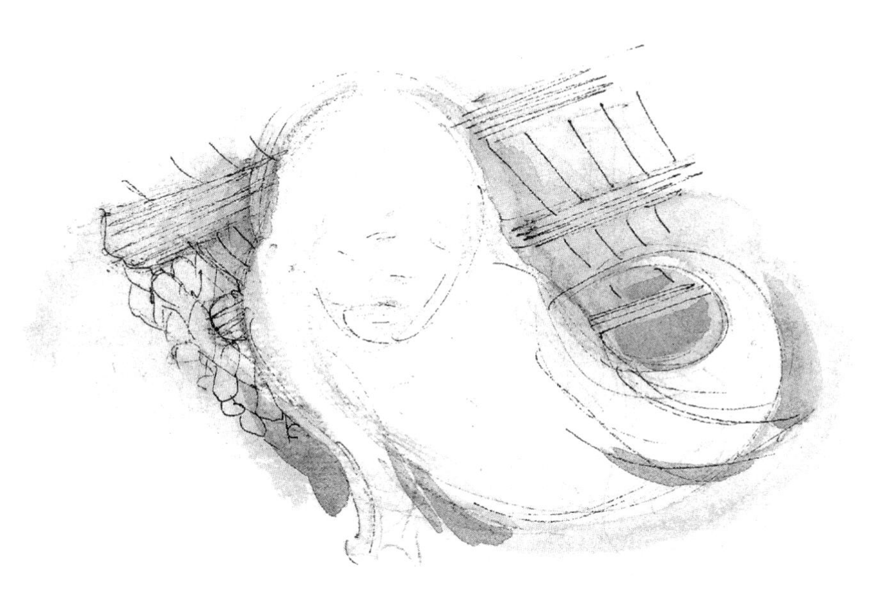

He missed his friend, Owl, like anything. Sadly, Gabriel crossed off the last day of October. "Home I shall go," decided Gabriel, "birthday or not."

"Yoo-hoo!" hooted a voice.

Gabriel flew to a window.

"Nice smells in the kitchen!" whispered Owl. "Paper swishing in the dining room! Children whispering all over town, too!"

"IT'S MY BIRTHDAY!" shouted Gabriel, heading for home at top speed.

At first, he thought he couldn't believe his eyes. Then he decided that he could. There were shining candles and orange-and-black streamers and frosty cakes and dishes of ice cream! There were jolly

jack-o'-lanterns at the windows and little bumpy presents at every plate! There were Mr. and Mrs. Gould, glowing like the candles on a cake! And, best of all, there were girls and boys, as full of fun as a lucky dip is full of surprises! And they were all dressed up like witches or owls or cats, or just like Gabriel himself!

"HAPPY HALLOWEEN!" called everybody.

"My birthday," thought Gabriel proudly, "even has a special name!" And at that, he sat right down with everybody else. Before very long, Gabriel decided that this was the most splendid birthday party that ever had been in the house at the edge of town.

The moon set late that night. At last Mr. and Mrs. Gould were sound asleep in their beds, and all the boys and girls were sound asleep in THEIR beds. At last Gabriel was alone in his little tower with all his lovely presents. There was a chain for Gabriel to rattle, a new sheet for Gabriel to wear for best, a paper hat that was just for fun, a jack-o'-lantern filled with nuts, and ever so many more things left around for Gabriel.

Just as the sun came up, which is when all good ghosts go to bed, Gabriel pulled the covers up under his chin.

"Goodnight, Owl," he called lovingly.

Softly, from the tree outside the window, Owl sang Gabriel a birthday song:

Happy Birthday to you-oooooo,
Happy Birthday to you-oooooo,
Happy Birthday, dear Gabriel,
Happy Birthday to you-oooooo!

The Errand

Susan Price

There was once a widow who had one son and one daughter, and she loved them both.

The daughter was courted by a merchant from a distant land who wanted to marry her and take her to live with him. The widow would not hear of it, because she could not bear to lose her daughter.

"Mother," said her son, "let my sister marry the man she loves, and I promise you that if you ever need her, I will travel to her husband's house and bring her back to you."

And, on this condition, the widow gave her permission for the marriage to take place.

The daughter went away to live in her husband's land, and there she was happy. She was visited, sometimes, by her mother and brother, and sometimes she visited them; and many letters and presents made the long journey between them.

One night the young woman was sitting by her parlor fire, reading. The clock had just struck midnight, but the story she read was so good that she lit another candle and read on. She was startled by a tapping at the window, and the sound of her name being called. She went to the window and looked out, and there stood her brother. He stared so fixedly at her and seemed so pale that she thought he must be ill. She opened the window and said, "Brother, what is the matter? Why are you here so late? Why didn't you write to me—why have you come?"

"Come," he said.

The girl could only think that her mother and brother had been on their way to visit her and there had been an accident.

She thought of her mother stranded somewhere near in the night, perhaps hurt, and she put a shawl about her shoulders and ran out of the house. Putting her hand into her brother's, she said, "Let us go to our mother."

Her brother's hand was cold as ice-water, and closed about hers with the tightest grip she had ever felt. He started away immediately, leading her along the road. They walked slowly, and yet the hills and trees slipped past as though they were flying. The woman could not be sure if they were really traveling so fast or if it was only the effect of the clouds covering and uncovering the moon.

They seemed to float on the moonlight and shadows like a light boat on swift water.

They came to a river and skimmed the trees and water shadows beside it. The young woman listened for a while to the sound of the river, and she said, "It's strange, but I hear words from the water, and it seems to be saying, 'See the living walk with the dead.' "

"You are in bed and dreaming," said her brother.

She laughed and said, "Perhaps I am."

They drifted on and passed beneath trees that arched high over the road and made the moonlight shiver as the breeze shook their leaves. "Listen," said

the young woman. "I hear the leaves speaking. They are saying, 'See the dead lead the living.' "

"You are asleep and dreaming," her brother repeated.

"I think I may be," she said.

On they went, the shadows flowing around them and growing more faint as morning approached. The young woman thought that she recognized the dimly seen hills as the hills of her native country, though she knew that she could not have come so far in a single night. All around them the birds began to wake and twitter, and she exclaimed, "Listen! I hear the birds talking, and

they are saying, 'See the living and the dead.' "

"You are asleep and dreaming," said her brother.

"I think I am," she said, as the day dawned, and she saw before her the city where she had been born. Her brother led her through the streets, through tunnels of brick walls. The windows shone in the first cold light, and all the birds sang. The bells of every church in the city were ringing, as they do for a death. The young woman was sure that she was dreaming—a bad dream, for on the door of house after house she saw painted the red cross that meant plague.

In her dream they reached the door of their

mother's house, and the young woman turned to her brother. She saw that his face was thinned to the bone and wretchedly pale. Before she could speak, he said, "Go in to our mother. Tell her I loved her, and that I kept my promise."

A cockerel crowed loudly, and her brother's hand melted from hers. He vanished like a shadow in light—and she knew then why her mother needed her.

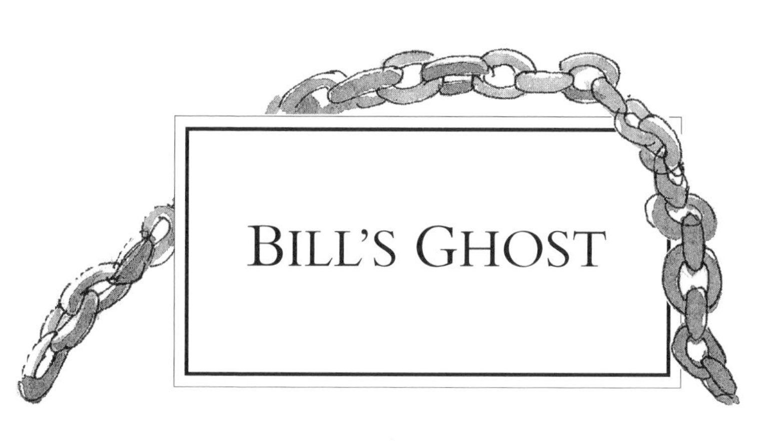

BILL'S GHOST

Catherine Storr

"So, just as you're going to sleep, you hear this noise," Bill said.

"What noise?"

"Clank, clank. Clank, clank, clank."

"Horrible noise. What is it?" Emily asked rapturously.

"Rusty chains."

"What's rusty chains for?"

"Rusty chains is what ghosts drag around with them."

"What's ghosts?" Emily asked.

"People who come back after they're dead and buried," Bill said.

Emily considered this. "What they come for?"

"They come at night and walk around your bed and groan. Like this." Bill produced a groan that started low and ended with a high-pitched wail.

He found it fairly frightening himself, but Emily was delighted with it and immediately tried to imitate it.

"I'm a ghost!" she said.

"You can't be. You're not dead. Anyway, you're much too fat to be a ghost. Ghosts are thin. And you can see right through them," Bill said.

"Like my fish?"

"No!" Bill shouted, exasperated.

"I can see through my fish. Sometimes. A bit."

"That's because of the kind of fish he is. You can't ever see through a person, not unless he's a ghost."

"Doesn't he wear any clothes? That's rude," Emily said.

"He wears armor. Like in the picture in the sitting-room. To fight in, so he doesn't get hurt. His armor clanks too."

"Clank, clank," Emily said, with gusto.

Bill felt that she was treating the subject too lightly. Ghosts were not meant to be enjoyed. He said, "He's had his head cut off."

"Is there blood?" Emily asked.

"Lots of blood. Dripping all over the place."

Emily sighed with pleasure.

"Where's his poor head, then?"

"Under his arm," Bill said.

"I can put my head under my arm," Emily said.

"Not like that, silly. With his arm at his side. Like this."

"I could do that too," Emily said.

"Not like he can. Because his head is cut off at the neck, see? So he can carry it like . . . like a football."

"Does it hurt?"

"It did when he had it cut off. You just think what it would be like if someone came along with a sword and chopped your head off."

"Poor head," Emily said.

"You'd scream."

"Wouldn't scream."

"Who wouldn't scream?" Bill's mother asked as she came into the room.

"Wouldn't if someone cut my head off," Emily said.

"What on earth have you been talking about?"

Bill said in a hurry, "About knights in armor, fighting." But he wasn't quick enough. His mother heard Emily say, "Poor ghosts you can see through like my fish."

"Bill! I've told you before, you're not to frighten Emily by telling her horrible stories just before she goes to bed."

"Horrible stories," Emily gloated.

"What did you say to her?" Bill's mother demanded.

"Blood dripping. Carries his head like a football," Emily said.

"Now, Emily! You're not to take any notice of what Bill was saying. All sensible people know there aren't any such things as ghosts," her mother said.

"No ghosts?" Emily asked.

"No, darling. No nasty ghosts."

Emily burst into tears.

"There! See what you've done! You've frightened her badly. It's all right, Emily, pet. Bill was just making it all up."

But Emily wouldn't be comforted. She was taken away by her mother to be bathed and fed with hot cocoa and sponge fingers before she was put to bed. Bill was left with the disagreeable promise that his mum would have something to say to him later. What made it all the more annoying was that he knew that what Emily was crying for was the abrupt end to the idea of ghosts with rusty chains and dripping necks. To be put back firmly into an ordinary world where only fish could be seen through and no one carried his head like a football under his arm, was too disappointing. Bill couldn't think why his mum was so anxious that he shouldn't frighten Emily. He'd never been able to do it yet.

Bill went to bed that night feeling sore. His mum had told him off, his dad had taken up the story and solemnly warned him against repeating the offense. He skipped his washing, in a don't-care mood, and went to bed at odds with the world. He wasn't supposed to read in bed in case he woke Emily, who shared his room. He lay gloomily in bed, thinking up tortures suitable for inconvenient younger sisters, until at last he fell, rather miserably, asleep.

He was woken by a noise he didn't recognize.

Not the swish of the passing car in the road outside. Not footsteps. Not the creak of the door, which meant that his mum was glancing in. Not the gentle scratching of Mrs. Twitchett, the cat, asking for a warm bit of a bed. Not the sound of rain on the roof. A noise like . . .

Clank. Clank. Clank.

"Who is it?" Bill asked. No one answered, but the something went Clank again, and there was a grating, metallic sound; it could have been the rattle of rusty chains being dragged along the ground.

Then there was a silence. It was complete, except for the hammering of Bill's heart, like waves pounding a shore; through it he could hear the tiny tick of his bedside clock. He could feel his hair standing up on his head. He was extremely frightened. However, he did not scream.

The room remained quite black and quiet.

Bill stretched out his hand to the table by his bed. His fingers closed over the torch he always had there. Almost the bravest thing he had ever done in his life was when he pressed the switch and shone the beam toward the place where those mysterious sounds had come from.

The batteries were old and it was a feeble ray of light. It was reflected back dimly from the unpolished armor of the breastplate and the plates covering the upper arms. Not from a helmet. Because above the shoulders the figure strangely ended with a very short neck. The head that should have topped the neck was being carried comfortably under the person's left arm. It was a good-looking head, with dark curly hair, a long nose, inquiring eyes, and a mouth curved in a distinctly friendly smile.

"Hi!" said the mouth.

Bill wasn't ready to answer this. The beam from the torch wavered slightly. Bill sat and gazed.

"Aren't you pleased to see me?" the mouth asked.

"I'm . . . Who are you?" Bill asked. He now noticed something else, very peculiar. Through the dim armor, through the agreeably conversing head, he distinctly saw the familiar furniture and the walls of his bedroom.

"You said to come, so I came. That's right, isn't it?" the mouth said, reproachfully.

"But . . ."

"I'm exactly like you said," the ghost said.

"But . . ."

"You can't say you weren't expecting me," the ghost said. He sounded disappointed, and Bill felt bad. But he couldn't get used to carrying on a conversation with a head worn so very much below the shoulders. He said, "Isn't it . . . Is it . . . uncomfortable having your head under your arm like that?"

"Agony," said the ghost, very cheerful indeed.

There was a short pause.

"Does it feel peculiar . . .? I mean does it feel funny to be . . . well, to be so that I can see right through you?" Bill asked.

The ghost was surprised. "Of course not. I'd have thought it would feel funny knowing that people can't see what's behind you. You must keep out an awful lot of light," the ghost said.

It was a nice idea to Bill. He said, "I suppose I'm used to it."

"Exactly. That's how I feel. I'm used to being the way I am," the ghost said. Another short pause.

"Oh! Sorry! I was forgetting," the ghost said suddenly. The mouth under the arm opened wide and groaned. It was a tremendous sound.

"Sh . . . ssssssh!"

"You wanted a groan," the ghost said, hurt.

"Yes, but . . . You might wake Emily."

"Is that Emily?" the ghost asked. The eyes in the head under the arm rolled toward the hump in Emily's bed.

"Yes. She's asleep. But if she wakes up and sees you, she'll scream."

The ghost moved over to look at Emily, clanking softly as he went.

"She's wearing her head on top too," he said, disappointed.

"Of course she is."

"I'd just hoped that one of you might look a bit more ordinary."

"Ordinary?"

"Like I am. With a see-through body and a head you can put anywhere you happen to want it, instead of having it always stuck in one place. It must be very boring."

"It isn't boring. You can always turn it around if you want to see something."

"Like this?" The ghost gave his detached head a spin, and it whirled like a top under his arm, eyes rolling. It made Bill feel dizzy to look at it.

"Not a bit like that," he said.

The head stopped spinning. "You'll be telling me next that you can't come and go as you please," the ghost said.

"What do you mean? Of course I can come and go."

"Like this?" the ghost asked. And disappeared.

Bill drew a breath of relief. But the relief didn't last. "Like this?" the ghost's voice said again. Bill turned his head—safely anchored on his neck—and saw the ghost standing on the farther side of Emily's bed.

"You can do that?" the ghost asked.

"Not quite like that. I just walk. Or run."

"Not quick enough," the ghost said.

"Not quick enough for what?" Bill asked.

"Well. Suppose we were talking, like we are now. And suppose the sun rose. I'd have to disappear. Double quick."

"Would you?" Bill asked hopefully.

"Don't worry. I reckon we've got another four hours yet. Or suppose someone else came into this room. I'd have to disappear then too. At once. No time to run. How could you manage that?"

Bill left this question unanswered. He said, "Why would you have to disappear if someone else came into the room?"

"My helmet, you are ignorant! Don't you really know that? I'm here because you believe in me. If someone came in who didn't believe in me, I'd have to go. See?"

Bill didn't entirely see. What he did understand, however, was that there might be a chance of dismissing the ghost before the sun rose. He couldn't stand another four hours of this, that was certain.

"You'd have to go and you wouldn't come back again?" he asked.

"Not unless I was sent for, like you sent for me this evening," the ghost said.

"It was very good of you to come," Bill said politely.

"It was a pleasure. And now you know how to

get in touch with me, I expect we'll be seeing a lot of each other. You can explain to me your peculiar way of living. What it's like to be so slow and so solid. I can't remember, it's such a long time since I was like that," the ghost said.

"Would you do something for me?" Bill asked.

"Anything," the ghost said warmly.

"I wish you'd groan again."

"You stopped me! You said to shush. Suppose I wake her?" The ghost's eyes turned to Emily again.

"I've just thought. She'd love to hear you," Bill said.

"Then certainly." The ghost rearranged his head and the mouth opened wide. The groan was blood-curdling. Bill felt a cold shiver run down his spine.

"How was that?" the ghost asked.

"Great! Please do it again."

The ghost gave another tremendous groan. Emily's sleeping form stirred.

"Enough?" the ghost suggested.

"Just one more," Bill pleaded.

The third groan was a magnificent performance. It was deeper and longer and louder than anything Bill could have produced. It was accompanied by the clank of rusty chains. If they hadn't just been having such a sane, if unusual, conversation, Bill could have believed that this was one of those historical ghosts, come to terrify and to bring bad news. He found the groan fairly frightening in spite of the friendliness of this agreeable ghost. He shut his eyes and hoped.

As the groan died away, there was a rustle from Emily's bed. The hump drew itself together, flattened out and rolled over. Emily's pink face rose over the bedclothes, eyes blinking, mouth open with surprise at what she saw.

She saw Bill, sitting up in bed, eyes shut, his torch in his hand. The beam was faint and flickering. It lit up the middle of her bed, a slanting patch of wall beyond, a chair with her clothes on it. It lit up nothing else.

She said, "You woke me!"

Bill's eyes flew open. He looked first at the other side of her bed. He said, "Emily?"

"What you looking at?"

Bill said, "Nothing. You can see, there's nothing there."

"Nothing there," Emily said.

"No. There isn't, is there?"

Emily wasn't interested in discussing nothing. She said, "You made a horrible noise."

"I didn't mean to," Bill said, not quite truthfully.

"You groaned."

"I'm not going to any more. Lie down and go to sleep again."

"You going to sleep?" Emily asked.

Bill said, "Yes," and switched off his torch to show that he meant it. He lay down. He heard Emily pull the bedclothes up as she lay down too.

"Dark," said Emily.

Bill hoped his sister was falling asleep in the

silence that followed. But suddenly a voice said, "Can't go to sleep."

"Shut your eyes."

"Tell me a story," Emily's voice said.

"No."

"Tell me about ghost."

"NO!"

"Poor ghost."

"Go to sleep, Emily."

"Wish ghost was real and would make clank, clank."

"Emily!"

"Tomorrow. Tell . . . about . . . ghost . . . blood . . . clank . . ." Emily's voice died out as sleep overcame her. Bill stayed awake for at least another five minutes, during which he made a firm resolution. Tell Emily, or anyone, about ghosts another time? As if he hadn't learned his lesson? Not if he knew it. Not ever again.

TOMMY AND THE GHOST

Kenneth Ireland

There once was a house that was so terribly haunted that no one could live in it.

Now there was a very simple kind old fellow, Old Tommy, living thereabouts who was said to have a way with ghosts. So the owner of the house sent for him and asked if he could lay it.

Tommy said he'd have a try if he'd give him an empty bottle and a cork to go with it, and a bottle of brandy and a tumbler to go with that.

So when night came he went into the house, lit a big fire in the grate, and sat down in a big chair in front of it to enjoy himself with the brandy.

Just as the clock struck twelve he heard a little noise, and there was the ghost standing beside him.

"Hello," said he to the ghost.

"Hello, Tommy," said the ghost. "And how are you?"

"Pretty well, thank you," Tommy replied politely. "But how do you know my name?"

"Oh, easy enough," said the ghost casually.

"But how did you get in?" asked Tommy. "It couldn't have been through the door, I'm sure of that."

"I got in through the keyhole," said the ghost.

"Nonsense! I can't believe it!"

"But I did," protested the ghost.

"I'd as soon believe that as believe a great fellow like you could get inside this empty bottle."

"But I can," said the ghost proudly.

"I don't believe that either," said Tommy.

"Then see if you can believe your own eyes," said the ghost.

And with that he drew himself down into the bottle.

As soon as he had, Tommy sealed it up safe and sound with the cork and took it down to the bridge over the river and threw it—*plunk!*—right under the middle arch.

And the house was never troubled again.

THE GHOST OF MISERY HILL

Robert D. San Souci

There was once a miner, Tom Bowers, who worked a claim on Misery Hill, near Pike City, in California. Tom was a loner: he never liked having people around him, he only went into town when he needed supplies, and he never took a partner. "Nobody's going to work my claim but me!" he told anyone who offered to buy into his claim.

During the winter he laid in supplies and kept to himself, while the snowdrifts piled up high around his cabin. People in Pike City always knew spring had arrived when Tom came down Misery Hill to purchase a fresh batch of foodstuffs.

But one spring, long after the last traces of snow had melted, the inhabitants of Pike City noticed that Old Tom hadn't turned up with his poke of gold dust to buy beans and salt pork, bread and coffee. After a good deal of discussion, a group of miners and townspeople rode off to investigate.

They found Tom's cabin empty; the pot-bellied stove was stone cold and some bits of fried bread had gone moldy in the big iron skillet on top of it. Clearly no one had been in the one-room shack for a long time.

Certain now that something had happened to the old miner, the men followed the path that ran from his cabin to the brink of the steep slope where he had done his prospecting. But they found the end of the trail had vanished—had been blotted out by a huge landslide.

Fearing the worst, they dug into the pile of earth and rock; and, after half a day of hard work, they found the old man's body. Then, having solved the mystery and having nothing better to do with Tom's remains, they buried him properly in a shallow grave not far from the mouth of his old mine shaft.

A few miners thought to work Tom's mine on Misery Hill, but the story soon grew that the ghost of Tom Bowers was often seen prowling around, carrying his old pick, near his mine. Soon everybody avoided the spot.

There was one miner, Jim Brandon, who got himself so far into debt when his own claim ran out that he became desperate. He moved into Tom's long-empty shack and began to work the abandoned mine. Soon enough he made it pay well enough to clear up his debts and accumulate a nest egg for himself.

But after several months, he began to notice signs that someone else was working his claim by night. Every morning he could see that somebody had tampered with the sluice—a long wooden trough he filled every day with freshly dug gravel. When water from a nearby stream was run down it, bars along the bottom of the sluice would catch any gold the gravel might hold.

Jim searched high and low for a clue to his

midnight visitor but found nothing. Thinking some of the other miners might be playing a trick on him, he challenged them. But they all swore they knew nothing about it.

After this, things were quiet for a few days. Then one morning, Jim again found that someone had been loading the sluice with gravel and running water through it. When evening came, he loaded his rifle and, hiding himself in a nook from which

he had a clear view of the claim site, he kept watch for the intruder.

For a long time he heard nothing but the wind whistling through the pines and the Yuba River rushing over rocks nearby. He could see the distant ridges of the Sierras gleaming in the starlight, but though he strained his eyes, he saw nothing moving near the mine entrance.

Then, by the light of the newly risen moon, he saw a notice shining on a nearby tree trunk, as though someone had just tacked it into place. Curious, he walked over and found the odd sign was as easy to read as if it was glowing by itself, not just reflecting the light of the full moon. It said:

Sure now that he was the victim of practical jokers, Jim grabbed for the paper to tear it down—only to feel an electric jolt run from his fingertips to his shoulder. His arm fell numbly at his side.

The notice vanished.

At the same time there came to his ears the sound of gravel being dumped into the sluice. A moment later he heard water gurgling into it, then the rattling and bumping of rocks being tumbled down the length of it.

Shaking his arm back into use, he angrily grabbed his gun and headed toward the sluice. Out of the corner of his eye, he saw the message was glowing again on the tree trunk, but he ignored it. He heard the sound of a pick biting into gravel, now, and nothing mattered except finding out what was going on.

Leveling his rifle, he rounded an outcrop of rock and saw Tom Bowers, swinging his pick near the entrance to the mine. The miner turned to glare at Jim, and the frightened man saw at a glance that he was a ghost. Tom's tall, skinny frame glowed just like the notice on the tree. His head and face were half-covered with lank, white hair; his eyes blazed from black sockets.

Scared nearly out of his wits, Jim raised his rifle to his shoulder and fired.

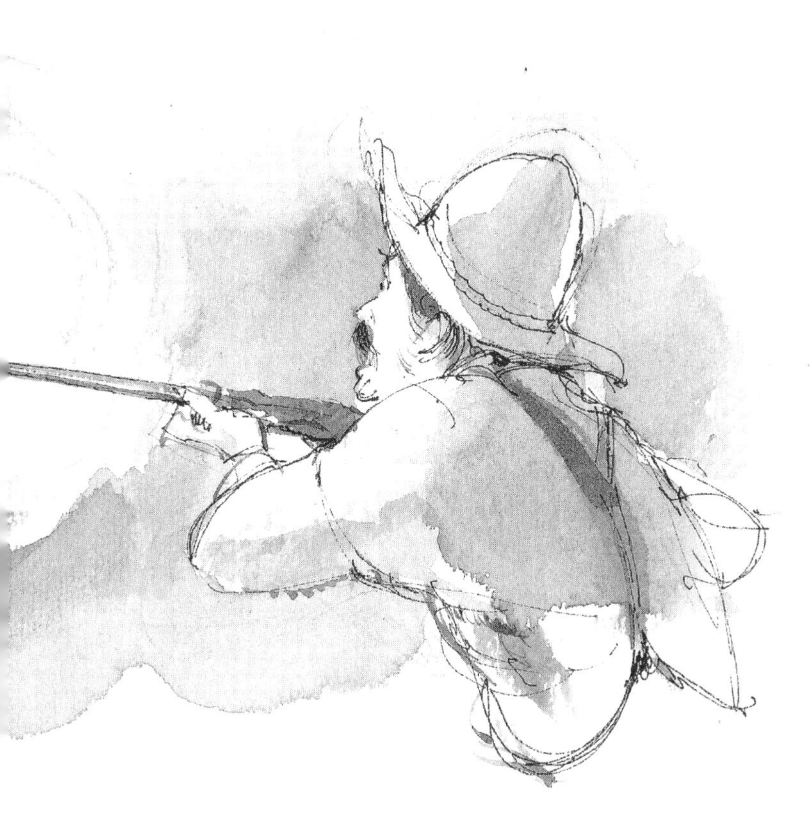

The gun's report was followed by a bellow from Tom's ghost. Looking through the rifle smoke, Jim saw the specter charging at him, his pick raised in both his hands.

"Oh, Lordy!" cried Jim and, still clutching his rifle, he took off running, with the angry ghost only a few paces behind.

The living led the dead a wild chase up hill and down, into and out of woods, over streams and ditches, and through scrub, toward Pike City.

In town the miners were all gathered in the saloon, celebrating a new gold strike. Suddenly everyone froze when they heard an ear-splitting scream. Then there was a sound like a body falling, followed by the clang of metal hitting on metal—then silence.

Everyone tumbled outside to see what had happened.

In the middle of the road, they found Jim Brandon's rifle pinned to the ground by the point of a pick sunk clean through the barrel. On the pick's handle were carved the initials "T.B."

No one ever saw Jim Brandon after that night. But for years afterward, miners working near Misery Hill reported the sluice at Tom Bowers's claim ran every night, just like clockwork.

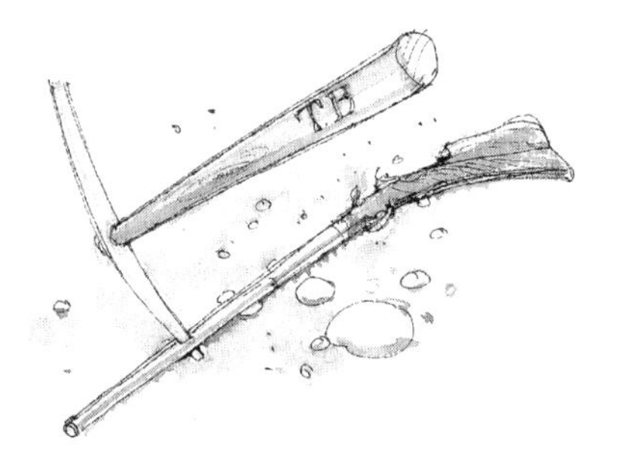

THE DAUNTLESS GIRL

Kevin Crossley-Holland

"Dang it!" said the farmer. "Not a drop left."

"Not one?" asked the blacksmith, raising his glass and inspecting it. His last inch of whisky glowed like molten honey in the flickering firelight.

"Why not?" said the miller.

"You fool!" said the farmer. "Because the bottle's empty." He peered into the flames. "Never mind that though," he said. "We'll send out my Mary. She'll go down to the inn and bring us another bottle."

"What?" said the blacksmith. "She'll be afraid to go out on such a dark night, all the way down to the village, and all on her own."

"Never!" said the farmer. "She's afraid of nothing—nothing live or dead. She's worth all my lads put together."

The farmer gave a shout and Mary came out of the kitchen. She stood and she listened. She went out into the dark night and in a little time returned with another bottle of whisky.

The miller and the blacksmith were delighted. They drank to her health, but later the miller said, "That's a strange thing, though."

"What's that?" asked the farmer.

"That she should be so bold, your Mary."

"Bold as brass," said the blacksmith. "Out and alone and the night so dark."

"That's nothing at all," said the farmer. "She'd go anywhere, day or night. She's afraid of nothing—nothing live or dead."

"Words," said the blacksmith. "But my, this whisky tastes good."

"Words nothing," said the farmer. "I bet you a golden guinea that neither of you can name

anything that girl will not do."

The miller scratched his head and the blacksmith peered at the golden guinea of whisky in his glass. "All right," said the blacksmith. "Let's meet here again at the same time next week. Then I'll name something Mary will not do."

Next week the blacksmith went to see the priest and borrowed the key of the church door from him. Then he paid a visit to the sexton and showed him the key.

"What do you want with that?" asked the sexton.

"What I want with you," said the blacksmith, "is this. I want you to go into the church tonight, just before midnight, and hide yourself in the dead house."

"Never," said the sexton.

"Not for half a guinea?" asked the blacksmith.

The old sexton's eyes popped out of his head. "Dang it!" he said. "What's that for then?"

"To frighten that brazen farm girl, Mary," said the blacksmith, grinning. "When she comes to the dead house, just give a moan or a holler."

The old sexton's desire for the half guinea was even greater than his fear. He hummed and hawed and at last agreed to do as the blacksmith asked.

Then the blacksmith clumped the sexton on the back with his massive fist and the old sexton coughed. "I'll see you tomorrow," said the blacksmith, "and settle the account. Just before midnight, then! Not a minute later!"

The sexton nodded and the blacksmith strode up to the farm. Darkness was falling and the farmer and the miller were already drinking and waiting for him.

"Well?" said the farmer.

The blacksmith grasped his glass, then raised it and rolled the whisky around his mouth.

"Well," said the farmer. "Are you or aren't you?"

"This," said the blacksmith, "is what your Mary will not do. She won't go into the church alone at midnight . . ."

"No," said the miller.

". . . and go to the dead house," continued the blacksmith, "and bring back a skull bone. That's what she won't do."

"Never," said the miller.

The farmer gave a shout and Mary came out of the kitchen. She stood and she listened; and later, at midnight, she went out into the darkness and walked down to the church.

Mary opened the church door. She held up her lamp and clattered down the steps to the dead house. She pushed open its creaking door and saw skulls and thigh bones and bones of every kind gleaming in front of her. She stooped and picked up the nearest skull bone.

"Let that be," moaned a muffled voice from behind the dead house door. "That's my mother's skull bone."

So Mary put that skull down and she picked up another.

"Let that be," moaned a muffled voice from behind the dead house door. "That's my father's skull bone."

So Mary put that skull bone down too and picked up yet another one. And, as she did so, she

angrily called out, "Father or mother, sister or brother, I *must* have a skull bone and that's my last word." Then she walked out of the dead house, slammed the door, and hurried up the steps and back up to the farm.

Mary put the skull bone on the table in front of the farmer. "There's your skull bone, master," she said, and started off for the kitchen.

"Wait a minute!" said the farmer, grinning and shivering at one and the same time. "Didn't you hear anything in the dead house, Mary?"

"Yes," she said. "Some fool of a ghost called out to me: 'Let that be! That's my mother's skull bone,' and 'Let that be! That's my father's skull bone.' But I told him straight: 'Father or mother, sister or brother, I *must* have a skull bone.'"

The miller and the blacksmith stared at Mary and shook their heads.

"So I took one," said Mary, "and here I am and here it is." She looked down at the three faces flickering in the firelight. "As I was going away," she said, "after I had locked the door, I heard the old ghost hollering and shrieking like mad."

The blacksmith and the miller looked at each other and got to their feet.

"That'll do then, Mary," said the farmer.

The blacksmith knew that the sexton must have been scared out of his wits at being locked all alone in the dead house. They all raced down to the church and clattered down the steps into the dead house, but they were too late. They found the old sexton lying stone dead on his face.

"That's what comes of trying to frighten a poor young girl," said the farmer. So the blacksmith gave the farmer a golden guinea and the farmer gave it to his Mary.

Mary and her daring were known in every house. And after her visit to the dead house, and the death of the old sexton, her fame spread for miles and miles around.

One day the squire, who lived three villages off, rode up to the farm and asked the farmer if he could talk to Mary.

"I've heard," said the squire, "that you're afraid of nothing."

Mary nodded.

"Nothing live or dead," said the farmer proudly.

"Listen then!" said the squire. "Last year my old mother died and was buried. But she will not rest. She keeps coming back into the house, and especially at mealtimes. Sometimes you can see her, sometimes you can't. And when you can't, you can still see a knife and fork get up off the table and play about where her hands would be."

"That's a strange thing altogether," said the farmer, "that she should go on walking."

"Strange and unnatural," said the squire. "And now my servants won't stay with me, not one of them. They're all afraid of her."

The farmer sighed and shook his head. "Hard to come by, good servants," he said.

"So," said the squire, "seeing as she's afraid of nothing, nothing live or dead, I'd like to ask your girl to come and work with me."

Mary was pleased at the prospect of such good employment and, sorry as he was to lose her, the farmer saw there was nothing for it but to let her go.

"I'll come," said the girl. "I'm not afraid of ghosts. But you ought to take account of that in my wages."

"I will," said the squire.

So Mary went back with the squire to be his servant. The first thing she always did was to lay a

place for the ghost at table, and she took great care not to let the knife and fork lie criss-cross.

At meals, Mary passed the ghost the meat and vegetables and sauce and gravy. And then she said: "Pepper, madam?" and "Salt, madam?" The ghost of the squire's mother was pleased enough. Things went on the same from day to day until the squire had to go up to London to settle some legal business.

Next morning, Mary was down on her knees, cleaning the parlor grate, when she noticed something thin and glimmering push in through the parlor door, which was just ajar; when it got inside the room, the shape began to swell and open out. It was the old ghost.

For the first time, the ghost spoke to the girl. "Mary," she said in a hollow voice, "are you afraid of me?"

"No, madam," said Mary. "I've no cause to be afraid of you, for you are dead and I'm alive."

For a while the ghost looked at the girl kneeling by the parlor grate. "Mary," she said, "will you come down into the cellar with me? You mustn't bring a light—but I'll shine enough to light the way for you."

So the two of them went down the cellar steps and the ghost shone like an old lantern. When they got to the bottom, they went down a passage and took a right turn and a left, and then the ghost pointed to some loose tiles in one corner. "Pick up those tiles," she said.

Mary did as she was asked. And underneath the tiles were two bags of gold, a big one and a little one.

The ghost quivered. "Mary," she said, "that big bag is for your master. But that little bag is for you, for you are a dauntless girl and deserve it."

Before Mary could open the bag or even open her mouth, the old ghost drifted up the steps and out of sight. She was never seen again and Mary had a devil of a time groping her way along the dark passage and up out of the cellar.

After three days, the squire came back from London.

"Good morning, Mary," he said. "Have you seen anything of my mother while I've been away?"

"Yes sir," said Mary. "That I have." She opened her eyes wide. "And if you aren't afraid of coming down into the cellar with me, I'll show you something."

The squire laughed. "I'm not afraid if you're not afraid," he said, for the dauntless girl was a very pretty girl.

So Mary lit a candle and led the squire down into the cellar, walked along the passage, took a right turn and a left, and raised the loose tiles in the corner for a second time.

"Two bags," said the squire.

"Two bags of gold," said Mary. "The little one is for you and the big one is for me."

"Lor!" said the squire, and he said nothing else. He did think that his mother might have given him the big bag, as indeed she had, but all the same he took what he could.

After that, Mary always crossed the knives and forks at mealtimes to prevent the old ghost from telling what she had done.

The squire thought things over: the gold and the ghost and Mary's good looks. What with one thing and another he proposed to Mary, and the dauntless girl, she accepted him. In a little while they married, and so the squire did get both bags of gold after all.

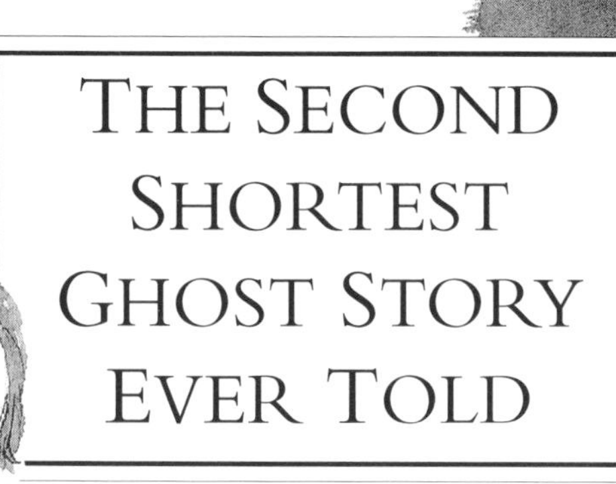

THE SECOND SHORTEST GHOST STORY EVER TOLD

Traditional

She was all alone in the old house.

Before she went to bed she made sure all the doors were locked. She latched the window and drew the curtains. She peered inside the closet and under the bed to make quite sure.

She undressed and put on her nightdress.

She got into bed. Then she reached out and switched off the light.

"Oh good," said a voice. "Now there are just the two of us."

TITLES IN THE TREASURY SERIES

ANIMAL STORIES

BEDTIME STORIES

CHRISTMAS STORIES

FUNNY STORIES

GHOST STORIES

GIANT AND MONSTER STORIES

IRISH STORIES

JEWISH STORIES

PONY STORIES

SPOOKY STORIES

STORIES FROM HANS CHRISTIAN ANDERSEN

STORIES FROM AROUND THE WORLD

STORIES FROM THE BROTHERS GRIMM

STORIES FROM THE OLD TESTAMENT

WITCHES AND WIZARDS

STORIES FOR FOUR YEAR OLDS

STORIES FOR FIVE YEAR OLDS

STORIES FOR SIX YEAR OLDS

STORIES FOR SEVEN YEAR OLDS

STORIES FOR EIGHT YEAR OLDS